HENRY JAMES

TURN OF THE
SCREW

ADAPTED BY
TIM LUSCOMBE

OBERON BOOKS
LONDON

WWW.OBERONBOOKS.COM

This adaptation first published in 2018 by Oberon Books Ltd
521 Caledonian Road, London N7 9RH
Tel: +44 (0) 20 7607 3637 / Fax: +44 (0) 20 7607 3629
e-mail: info@oberonbooks.com
www.oberonbooks.com

A catalogue record for this book is available from the British Library.

PB ISBN: 9781786826114
E ISBN: 9781786826121

eBook conversion by CPI Group (UK) Ltd, Croydon, CR0 4YY.

Visit www.oberonbooks.com to read more about all our books and to buy them.
You will also find features, author interviews and news of any author events, and
you can sign up for e-newsletters so that you're always first to hear about our new
releases.

10 9 8 7 6 5 4 3 2 1

Dealing with ambiguity in adapting Henry James' *The Turn of the Screw*

Henry James's novella *The Turn of the Screw* has already been adapted many times, providing the source material for several films, two full-length ballets, by Will Tucket and Luigi Zaninelli, an opera by Benjamin Britten and a play on Broadway directed by Harold Pinter. It's inspired retellings and reimaginings and prequels and sequels, including Joyce Carol Oates' *The Accursed Inhabitants of House Bly* – one of the latest examples of a writer taking James' narrative and making it her own. Michael Winner's *The Nightcomers* and Alejandro Amenábar's *The Others* are acclaimed instances of the same approach in film, though Jack Clayton's more faithful *The Innocents* remains the most generally celebrated.

The novella, originally published between January and April 1898 in twelve parts in *Collier's Weekly*, a New York illustrated magazine, began life in fact as a story told to James by the Archbishop of Canterbury on a summer evening in 1895 in the archbishop's palace near Croydon. The archbishop was passionately interested in ghosts and ghost phenomena, and so was James. Actually, the tale, if it can be credited with a creator, properly belongs to the woman who'd initially related it to the archbishop. The events – innocent children being haunted and corrupted by ghosts – actually happened, she claimed, to members of her own family. According to James' journal, though, the poor woman had told the events of the visitations badly and incompletely. At any rate, it was enough to inspire the novelist two years later to want to flesh it out and create something gripping and commercial, each of the twelve episodes ending in a thrilling cliff-hanger climax and helping to increase sales of the magazine.

The structure of the novella is similarly bracketed, with storyteller quoting storyteller, and involves an identical imbalance of gender. The instigating 'I' listens to a man called Douglas read aloud a story (around a fire at Christmas time) that had been related to him by a woman employed as a governess in a country house in Bly, Essex (she's dead at the time Douglas tells her story). The governess has been tasked with looking after two orphaned children since their uncle in London is too pre-occupied with enjoying himself to do so.

James' introduction distances the woman's voice, protecting it, or perhaps censoring it, in any case screening it with two others – three if you count James as well. Incidentally, James suffered from what we now know as carpal tunnel syndrome and couldn't write the novel himself, or type it, but instead had to dictate it to his secretary, thus adding another filter to the process.

In my adaptation, I omit all these parenthetical story-telling devices and give the governess a stage on which to tell her tale uncluttered by male interpreters.

Though I evaded the need to find a stage-worthy solution to James' narrative tricks, the sense, in the original, of a story within a story within a story at least creates distance from the soul-shaking events contained therein. Its Christmas setting seems to suggest that the tale – however scary – might best be regarded as only a piece of entertainment, prompting us to wonder whether perhaps we needn't give it too much credence. It's just a ghost story. Not a word of it is actually true. And yet, in their day, the archbishop and the novelist were not unusual in their belief in the existence of spirits.

Practically debunked today, investigation of spirit phenomena was regarded as a science in late Victorian England. A group of Cambridge academics, led by a professor of moral philosophy, researched and documented hundreds of ghost sightings. James himself was a member of the Society for Psychical Research, which grew out of the Cambridge group, and his brother William, a Harvard psychologist, was for a time its president. Shortly before writing *The Turn of the Screw*, James spoke at a meeting of the Society, reading aloud a report about a woman named Mrs Piper, a spirit medium whose body and voice seemed at times to be employed by the spirit of a dead man. Indeed, the physical descriptions in the novella of the ghost-characters of Peter Quint and Miss Jessel owe a great deal to the descriptions of ghosts appearing to James' contemporaries, whose personal experiences and reports he studied.

Yet, very few, at least since Edmund Wilson's 1934 essay on *The Ambiguity of Henry James*, have believed that James's ghost story is merely a ghost story. Over the last hundred years, more than five hundred books and essays in English alone have attempted to pinpoint and identify the nature of the evil in the work. And these critical studies have centred around the question of whether the ghosts are in fact ghosts – are, in fact, actual apparitions that present themselves to the governess – and the concomitant question, if the ghosts are not real, of whether the governess is mad. Actually, the scholarship on James' novella seems to have taken on a life of its own, producing a vast amount of readings at least as broad ranging, controversial and contradictory as any of the work's wilder stage, film and novelistic adaptations.

On the surface, *The Turn of the Screw* is simply a ghost story told by a governess recounting events that happened to her. However, once you reach the end of her tale and find her holding the body of a dead boy and you grapple with her reaction to it, it's inevitable that you begin to wonder about her reliability as a narrator. On second reading, you look for inconsistencies, hints of her mendacity, and perhaps you start to discern that she's driven by more than a need to protect the children, that she is, in fact, deranged by sexual urges she can't understand or act upon. That, at any rate, is what I began to understand. And it was at this point I comprehended what I was up against when it came to adapting the work to stage.

The commissioning producer had specifically tasked me with retaining the ambiguity of the original. Well, the profusion of ambiguity didn't present a problem. Instead, the challenge became how to find a way to balance every character and every piece of action in order to allow the audience to make up its own mind about what's really going on. For, while a novel can be written in the first person singular, a play is always played in the third person, singular or plural. In other words, I had to tell the story in a way that, when played by actors and viewed by an audience, could offer any number of conceivable interpretations.

However hard I tried not to, though, I still felt the need to reach decisions about James' underlying intentions. One day, it seemed to me, the ghosts were real, the next not. One day the governess was a brave young woman brim full of integrity and love for her charges, the next a murdering psychotic. How could I, I cried with mounting desperation, tell a story in which the ghosts are real and not real, in which the governess is mad and not mad? And my bafflement didn't end there. Are the children, I needed to know, innocent? Have they been corrupted by the ghosts? How does Mrs Grose know, from the governess' description, that the first apparition the governess sees is that of Peter Quint? How exactly does the boy die? Is this a story of sexual coercion and, if so, of what nature? Heterosexual, homosexual, or paedophilic? I still had no idea how to read the story in the 'best' way and therefore no real clue about how to adapt it into a strong, clear theatrical narrative.

Hardly helping to unclutter my vision were the many academic readings of the novella which used, among others, psychoanalysis, feminism, deconstructionism and Marxism as models of interpretation. Each seemed, to a mind eager for a 'solution', highly credible. For instance, in Brice Robbins' brilliant Marxist analysis (*"They don't much count, do they?": The Unfinished History of The Turn of the Screw*), Robbins reads the novella in terms of class warfare and argues that the real ghosts in the uncle-plutocrat's country mansion are the servants, and points to Miles' heroism in refusing "to play along with the wilful blindness of his class that consigns the servants to willed, organized invisibility – that makes them all ghostly..." Seductively (in my opinion), Robbins goes on to state that, "thanks to their bizarre isolation, raised by servants alone, without interference from the upper classes, the children have become little democrats, unable to see the sin in transgressing those class divisions that the adult world takes for granted".

By the same token, I found Stanley Renner's directly opposed psychoanalytical essay *"Red hair, very red, close curling": Sexual Hysteria, Physiognomic Bogeymen, and the 'Ghosts' in The Turn of the Screw* equally credible. With similar authority, Renner asserts that what James actually wanted to say when he wrote the story was "that the angel in the house [i.e. the governess] might really be an angel of psychic destruction, votary of an ideal moving through society from house to house doing mortal damage to human sexual development" and that the novelist "produced a ghost story that would materialize…as one of the most remarkable psychological dramas in literature… A story about the damage done to the sexual development of children by Victorian sexual fear and disgust…"

For a time, prompted by Renner, I fell in with the idea that *The Turn of the Screw* is, in fact, for those with the stomach to face it, a story revealing James' own psychosexual childhood traumas, and his writing of it an act of revenge against the various castrating women of his youth.

There would, after all, be many reasons for James to write a message subliminally if it dared concern itself with sex. Fred Kaplan, one of his biographers, tells us that James was merely a passive and repressed observer and terrified of sex. Something many agree on is that he shared the prudish Victorian view that physical aspects of human passion (of any kind) were out of place in serious fiction. But, even had he not been so cautious from the point of view of literary taste, we might remember that in 1895 – the year in which the archbishop furnished James with the idea for the story – Oscar Wilde was sentenced to two years hard labour for homosexual offences. As Peter G Beidler points out, equally fresh in James' mind must have been "the storm of opprobrium that had befallen Thomas Hardy when he ventured to criticize Victorian sexual sanctities – showing, for example, through Tess that a sexual lapse did not really commit a girl to hopeless depravity, and through Jude that the spiritual-love ideal could turn marriage into a torment for people with normal sexual desires".

It seemed more and more obvious to me that, in a profoundly coded way, *The Turn of the Screw* was an attack on Victorian family values, the cult of the governess and perhaps, even more controversially, an attempt to address the taboo subject of homosexuality, and that therefore, as its adaptor, I should find a way of expressing this. And yet how could I be sure I'd hit upon the 'right' reading? As soon as I turned back to the Marxists, it was once again perfectly obvious to me that the crime for which

Miles is expelled from his school, for passing onto his friends some unpardonable and unsayable information, was not to do with a sense of his burgeoning if unconventional sexuality, but it was the truth he'd learned from Quint – the radical concept that servants are as valuable as anyone else, and that the upper classes were in terminal moral decline.

So baffled by critical scholarship, I returned to the biographies where one fact is strikingly clear. The 1890s was a bad time for James. Only five years before he began work on *The Turn of the Screw*, his beloved sister Alice, who'd been preoccupied with suicide and suffered from mental ill health throughout her life, had died following a lingering illness. (Alice, in fact, might well be considered the prime source of inspiration for the governess). A year after her death, James turned fifty, suffered a severe attack of gout and wrote to a friend that he was "moody, misanthropic, melancholy, morbid [and] morose". Another friend, to whom he was very attached, committed suicide a year after that. But not only did he have to contend with emotional pain, James' books weren't selling well either, and an attempt to make money from playwriting was proving to be a spectacular flop. The London audiences thought his theatrical efforts too 'talky' and too 'refined', and the most lauded only played for a month in London. His older brother William, conversely, was rising to international prominence as America's greatest authority on the new subject of psychology. So I imagine it was with a sense of having nothing much to lose that James embarked on the adventure of writing something true to life (which was, after all, his ambition for literature) and to his particular experience of it. In January 1895 he wrote, 'It is now indeed that I may do the work of my life, and I will!' And one of the first things he produced shortly after was *The Turn of the Screw*.

It's not hard to see the themes of his situation and of the novella reflecting each other: unreturned love, unappreciated talent, death, abandonment, innocence corrupted and evil. As Beidler summarises, "James mined the previous five years of death, sickness and failure to produce one of his most popular and successful works."

If I ever felt close to discovering how to proceed in putting all that I now knew into an adaptation of the ghost story, it was when I learned that some scholars, equally baffled by the mire created by their colleague's contradictory thought, had reached the conclusion that to decide what the work meant was beside the point. Structuralist and deconstructionist thinkers, such as Tzvetan Todorov, Jacques Lacan and Jacques Derrida, just like Boris Johnson's designs on Brexit, argued that it was perfectly possible to achieve a 'cake and eat it' interpretation. Todorov's view, for instance, is that *The Turn of the Screw* "does not permit us to determine finally whether the ghosts haunt the old estate, or whether we are confronted by the hallucinations of a hysterical governess victimised by the disturbing atmosphere that surrounds her". "There is no word or incident in the story that cannot be interpreted both ways", argued experimental novelist Christine Brooke-Rose. And, as John Carlos Rowe maintained, "We cannot know… We are forever dupes of the language that employs us".

From these writers, I gained the confidence to go forward in the knowledge that the 'right' approach was one which attempted to mimic James' awe-inspiring talent for providing action, characterization and dialogue which, in every case, allows multiple interpretations to exist simultaneously and which has yielded scholars the material to inspire their analysis to flourish in every conceivable direction. It's not that one thing or the other is happening, it's that both are happening at the same time. The ambiguity of James' writing is such that it allows you to hold two opinions at once.

When I met the director of the production to discuss the script, I wasn't surprised that his first question to me was to know what I imagined actually happens in the story. He'd been on the same journey as me and was very conscious, come the first day of rehearsal, that the actors and creative team would be asking him the same question. Naturally enough, he wished to know what I had in mind. Regretfully, I had to tell him, even after working on the script for many months, that I still don't know for sure, but that, naturally, he's free, if not obliged, to make up his *own* mind, as long, that it, as the production honestly attempts to avoid coming down too heavily on one side or the other – that, in other words, it allows the audience to decide for themselves.

So, what *actually* happens?

You tell me.

Tim Luscombe, July 2017

This introduction is adapted from an essay that was published in Volume 39, Issue 3 of *Henry James Review*. © 2018, Johns Hopkins University Press.

My thanks go to Dorothea Löbbermann for the inspiring conversations

Turn of the Screw by Henry James, adapted by Tim Luscombe, adaptation conceived by Dermot McLaughlin, was first produced by Dermot McLaughlin Productions with Mercury Theatre Colchester and Wolverhampton Grand Theatre, premiering on 23rd February 2018. The cast was as follows:

THE GOVERNESS	Carli Norris
MRS CONRAY	Annabel Smith
MRS GROSS	Maggie McCarthy
THE MAN	Michael Hanratty
Understudy/ASMs	Jen Holt
	Tom MacQueen

The Tour

Mercury Theatre, Colchester, 23 Feb – 10 March
Theatre Royal, Windsor, 13 – 17 March
West Yorkshire Playhouse, Leeds, 20 – 24 March
Malvern Festival Theatre, 27 – 31 March
New Theatre Royal, Plymouth, 3 – 7 April
Grand Theatre, Wolverhampton, 10 – 14 April
Connaught Theatre, Worthing, 18 – 21 April
Yvonne Arnaud Theatre, Guildford, 24 – 28 April
Theatr Clwyd, Mold, 1 – 5 May
Pomegranate Theatre, Chesterfield, 8 – 12 May
Devonshire Park Theatre, Eastbourne, 15 – 19 May
New Theatre, Cardiff, 22 – 26 May

Dermot McLaughlin is the proud recipient of Stage One Bursary and Start Up awards for *Turn of the Screw*.

To find out more about Stage One's programmes, please visit www.stageone.uk.com

STAGE
ONE
TRAINING PRODUCERS IN THEATRE
FOR YEARS

Characters

Four actors – three female & one male – play

THE GOVERNESS

MRS CONRAY/FLORA

MRS GROSE

THE EMPLOYER, MILES and THE OTHERS

It's too horrible.

For sheer terror?

For dreadful...dreadfulness! For uncanny ugliness and horror and pain.

Oh, how delicious!

Notes

THE TIME

Although, the play starts in 1870, most of the action takes place in 1840.

THE GOVERNESS

Through 1840, in accordance with the governess' changing perception of Flora and Miles, her two charges age from 8 and 11 respectively in the summer to become more or less adult by the winter. For the same reason, the 'Others' (Peter Quint and Miss Jessel) should be rendered differently as time progresses. They're wildly scary at the beginning, becoming less so as the action moves forward, almost tameable when the governess outfaces one of them, and finally invisible – in line with her fracturing sanity (and in accord with the audience's growing doubt about her credibility).

THE CHANGES

Because, for three of the actors, the action involves so much rapid morphing (of age and/or character), I suggest simplicity is the key, shedding or gaining decades or switching characters at the drop of a non-literal hat. Such a functional story-telling style refuses complicated costume changes, and, instead, relies on actors' 'turn-on-a-dime' transformational skills and an audience's enjoyment of witnessing them. It also serves the nonstop nature of the narrative. (Although there are scene divisions, the action within an act should never stop for costume or scene changes).

However, this minimal presentational style won't do for the Others.

THE OTHERS

The first few appearances of the Others should be properly chilling moments, with no effort spared to make a bold theatrical impact. The production's creative team must 'turn the screw' on the scare factor to as great a degree as possible, within inevitable restrictions arising from two key facts:

1. Some of the changes for the (male) actor, who plays both of the Others, are extremely rapid, and

2. One of the Others is a woman. A black veil might be a solution – and it would fit Miss Jessel's character.

THE DESIGN

There's an emotional and physical hothouse atmosphere pervading the novella. The characters are continually hugging, kissing, embracing and clutching at each other, and more or less every one calls everyone else 'my dear'. It's not camp, but respectful and easy and in line with the physical exuberance of the period. Additionally, Henry James uses it to maintain intense emotionality and show both how blurred the lines between peoples' identities are, and how inappropriate intimacy can become the norm in a closed and unregulated community.

'It was striking of the children, at all events, to kiss me inveterately with a kind of wild irrelevance'. (Henry James, 'Turn of the Screw').

It would be terrific if this cloying steaminess could somehow be reflected in the design as well as in the playing.

THE CASTING

It's intended that the audience understands that the children are not played by actual children. The skill of the two actors playing them must help the audience accept the fact, while convincing them it's not true.

THE FURNITURE

This adaptation was written for a mid-scale touring production, so it's imagined that, for example, the drapes, the mirror, the mysterious portrait and the employer's trophies are placed out-front. What *is* actually needed are: two chairs and a desk for Mrs Conray's drawing room, and, to suggest a variety of rooms and locations within Bly, there should be (at least) some schoolroom furniture, a rocking horse, a rocking chair, a hall table and a bed. The bed needn't be big, and is deemed to belong to whoever's occupying it at the time.

THE PUNCTUATION

At the end of a speech:

When there's a dash (–), the next speaker interrupts.

When there are three dots (…), the thought dribbles away, uninterrupted,

But, in the middle of a line, those same punctuation marks can mean various other things.

Act One

Pre-set reveals two acting areas with no sharp division between them. To one side of the stage is Mrs Conray's drawing room in 1870, but taking up the bulk of the playing area is Bly, a country house, in 1840. Bly's furniture is covered in dustsheets. Taken altogether, what can be seen of the pleasant set hints at nothing darker than Victorian wealth and good taste.

SCENE ONE.

However, when house lights dim, sound begins to suggest a much darker, scarier world with the fluttering of birds' wings and children's laughter mixed in with jarring word-blurts and unsettling, increasingly crazed music. It builds. The lights have become shadowy when a dustsheet in Bly is pulled back, apparently unaided. A child's rocking horse starts to move of its own volition, as if there were a person riding it. But there's no one. Music and sound build to a terrifying crescendo and, at their peak, lights snap out.

SCENE TWO.

1870

When lights are quickly restored, the rocking horse is motionless, and the focus has shifted to Mrs Conray's sunny suburban drawing room in a well-to-do part of North London. City birds can be heard singing in the leafy street outside.

MRS CONRAY, 38-years-old, escorts another woman – a prospective GOVERNESS – into the room. Mrs Conray is outwardly smooth but capable of sudden sharpness. The prospective GOVERNESS manages to hide a neurotic disposition under a cloak of studied self-assurance – at least initially.

MRS CONRAY: Take a seat, won't you?

The GOVERNESS occupies the less elaborate of two chairs, and faces MRS CONRAY across a desk.

(Continued, consulting references.) Who doesn't know that a gentleman should never ask a lady her age, but I'm unaware of any rule preventing another lady from doing so. So, my dear, if *you*'ve no objection…?

GOVERNESS: None at all, Mrs Conray. I'm fifty years old.

MRS CONRAY: *(Doing some quick mental arithmetic.)* Good. Your marital status?

GOVERNESS: M…? Oh I'm unmarried, naturally.

The GOVERNESS nervously rubs the inside of her left wrist with her thumb.

MRS CONRAY: The references are exemplary. Mrs Whittock says, in terms of supervising her children's welfare and education, you demonstrated supreme skill; your service to Mrs Hawk's household – matchless; and Mrs Ashmore, who initially directed me to you, describes the most agreeable woman she's ever known in your position – that you would, in fact, be worthy of any whatever. I see no reason, if you're willing to take charge of my three little darlings, to prevent you from doing so.

GOVERNESS: I'd be delighted.

MRS CONRAY: You mightn't be when you've met them. They're horrors, every one.

GOVERNESS: Oh I've experienced plenty of real horrors. I'm sure yours will provide no fresh challenge.

MRS CONRAY: Despite the brevity of this interview, my offer isn't made lightly. I'm aware that the importance of a governess in the development of a child's mind and body can hardly be overstated. I've often thought the governesses of England play as vital a role in maintaining our Empire as the government.

The GOVERNESS is amused and flattered.

(Continued.) I had one myself, of course, and she shaped me… Well, her influence on my life was profound. Now my only desire would be to know a little more about you. Your background.

The GOVERNESS unconsciously rubs her left wrist again.

GOVERNESS: Of course, Mrs Conray. Though I can't imagine…Nothing about my life is so very remarkable.

MRS CONRAY: You weren't originally a Londoner.

GOVERNESS: Oh no, I was born in Hampshire.

MRS CONRAY: And your father?

GOVERNESS: Was a parson.

MRS CONRAY: And you began work at what age?

GOVERNESS: The age of twenty.

MRS CONRAY: I see.

GOVERNESS: Mrs Conray, I can't believe you've any interest in –

MRS CONRAY: *(Interrupting.)* For whom? *(Pleasant again.)* For whom?

GOVERNESS: I beg your pardon?

MRS CONRAY: Who was your first employer?

GOVERNESS: It was such a long time ago –

MRS CONRAY: Nevertheless, her name?

GOVERNESS: I feel I'm being cross-examined.

3

MRS CONRAY: Her name, if you please.

GOVERNESS: I can't remember the name.

MRS CONRAY: Surely – your very first engagement –

GOVERNESS: But why? Are you unsatisfied with my references?

MRS CONRAY: They're nonpareil, but if I'm to trust you with my schoolroom and nursery, I wish to hear about your early experiences as well as the most recent. It must have been daunting at twenty to take charge of the welfare of young of children. A provincial girl – not sophisticated or even knowledgeable I presume. A formidable task.

GOVERNESS: *(Increasingly uncomfortable, and unable to hide it.)* I don't understand. Have you heard something that... My references –

MRS CONRAY: *(A flash of aggression.)* Damn the references. I wish to hear you speak about your early employment.

GOVERNESS: I'm afraid that's really very...Well, I'm afraid I can't comply, Mrs Conray.

MRS CONRAY: Why ever not?

GOVERNESS: You're correct. When I began work as a governess I was unsophisticated and I made many mistakes. But one might hope to be forgiven and permitted... I see no reason to revisit those, that, period. After my first engagement, for a time I stopped working. I spent a while in... Well, I was, I wasn't fully well. But when I was judged to have recovered, I worked again as a governess and have worked ever since, and to my knowledge that work has not merited a single complaint...

MRS CONRAY waits.

(Continued, rising.) I think, in fact, I, I, I'd prefer to leave. I'm sorry to have taken up your afternoon and disappointed you.

MRS CONRAY: Sit down.

The GOVERNESS tries to leave, but MRS CONRAY stops her.

(Continued.) You fail to understand. I will be answered. I will have the name of your first employer.

GOVERNESS: You will allow me to pass –

MRS CONRAY: Sit down!

The GOVERNESS is made to sit. She grasps her left wrist, and puts it to her mouth, her breathing becoming short.

(Continued.) I'll give you a clue.

GOVERNESS: What do you want?

MRS CONRAY: Your first employer was, in fact, a young man in London.

The GOVERNESS is shocked. She rubs her left wrist against her neck.

(Continued.) Ah, light dawns. Or should I say a shadow falls. A dashing young man in Weymouth Street –

GOVERNESS: In God's name, who are you?

A dashing young man enters.

MRS CONRAY: …who placed an advertisement in the press requesting the services of a governess, and, neither experienced nor travelled, you answered it –

The GOVERNESS has risen, shedding three decades and all her neurotic twitches. So it's a fluttered, anxious and eager virgin, never before in the capital, who approaches her potential first employer.

SCENE THREE.

1840

Weymouth Street.

EMPLOYER: Yes, it was almost exactly two years ago that my
  brother, poor chap, passed away.

GOVERNESS: Oh how awful –

*The EMPLOYER is determined to make an impression and knows
how to do so.*

EMPLOYER: Yes, he and his wife were out in India. Both
  succumbed to typhoid. Damned water was contaminated.
  What they tell me.

*As well as being thoroughly impressed by the young man, the
GOVERNESS can't help but be distracted by the room, overwhelmed
by its size and magnificence.*

(Continued.) And there was no one else. No other relation.
  The upshot? I became sole guardian to my niece and
  nephew, little Flora and Miles. Bad luck for them, eh?

He laughs and she copies.

(Continued.) Well, at first, the whole thing was a great
  worry. Naturally I wished to do what I could for the
  poor chicks, but I'm alone, you understand, with neither
  the right sort of experience nor, to be frank, a grain of
  patience for such things.

He laughs, she copies.

(Continued.) So I sent them down to Bly, my other house.
  I thought the country really the proper place for children.
  I went down myself a few times to see how they were
  getting on, took a couple of my best people with me to
  help out, my valet and so on, but my affairs here take up

all my time as you can no doubt imagine, and I travel a good deal.

GOVERNESS: Yes. *(Admiring his trophies.)* Such extraordinary items…

He straddles a chair.

EMPLOYER: So, my dear, if you took the post, you'd be in supreme authority at Bly – in charge of the children naturally, as well as the below-stairs people. There's a housekeeper, Mrs Grose – my mother's old maid – immensely capable. There's a cook, a couple of housemaids, an old pony, a gardener, and Luke the errand boy. Little Flora's at home all the time, and Miles… Well, we had the misfortune to lose our last governess. *(Responding to her inquisitive expression.)* Yes. A most respectable young woman, very like yourself – managed the children quite beautifully, but unfortunately she…died.

The GOVERNESS is shocked.

(Continued.) It was all, to be frank, greatly awkward, and meant that I had to arrange a school for the boy. He's young of course, but I didn't know what else to do. Anyway, he'll be coming home for the summer holiday any day now. You look worried. Does the prospect strike you as terribly dull – all serious duty and no company? *(Bringing his chair closer.)* I see it in your face.

GOVERNESS: Well…

EMPLOYER: It's true that for several applicants, the conditions have seemed prohibitive. But Bly is a very cheerful place, you know, and healthy and secure. I'm certain for a fact you'd get on tremendously well with Mrs Grose. *(Closer.)* And, my dear, your acceptance of my offer would do me, personally, such a very great favour. I would be *(Kissing her hand.)* forever in you debt. *(Looking into her eyes.)* I'd gratefully incur such an obligation to you. *(He sits back in his chair, sprawling magnificently.)*. In fact, I'd be prepared, in addition to board and lodging, to pay you a pound and ten shillings a week.

The GOVERNESS looks even more shocked, this time positively.

(Continued.) Now, what do you say?

MRS CONRAY interrupts from 1870.

MRS CONRAY: What *could* you say, so charming as he was.

GOVERNESS: *(Entranced.)* Oh yes.

MRS CONRAY: How persuasive.

GOVERNESS: Very, oh very.

MRS CONRAY: And such a way with a woman.

GOVERNESS: I accept.

EMPLOYER: You do? That's splendid. Then it's to Bly I'd like you immediately to proceed.

GOVERNESS: Very well.

EMPLOYER: There's just one further condition.

GOVERNESS: *(Innocently.)* What?

EMPLOYER: That you should never trouble me –

GOVERNESS: – oh –

EMPLOYER: – never, neither appeal nor complain nor write to me about anything. You'll meet all questions yourself – you'll receive all moneys from my solicitor – you'll take the whole thing over and let me alone.

GOVERNESS: I promise I will. And I promise...

EMPLOYER: What?

GOVERNESS: You won't be disappointed in me.

EMPLOYER: My dear, you have taken a huge weight off my shoulders. *(Holding her hand.)* Thank you sincerely for the sacrifice you're making for my family. The sacrifice you make for me.

The GOVERNESS is in love.

The employer abruptly exits.

SCENE FOUR.

1870

MRS CONRAY calls the GOVERNESS back to 1870 to reveal who she really is.

MRS CONRAY: My uncle *still* has a very considerable way with women.

GOVERNESS: Your...?

MRS CONRAY: Not as gallant as he was thirty years ago of course –

GOVERNESS: You mean?

MRS CONRAY: But tremendously charming, even now.

A fluttering of wings as the birds in the street all take flight at once.

GOVERNESS: Oh, God! I see it...

MRS CONRAY is in fact FLORA, one of the GOVERNESS's first charges, now in middle age.

FLORA: When I was growing up, he never spoke about what happened. I was never particularly close to him. I was eight – too young to remember – and I never enquired. As a child one senses – doesn't one? – when a subject is out of bounds. And now he's dying. It's the only explanation I have for the fact that, after all these years, he wishes to discuss... Well, he's even started to wonder – perhaps the old chap's losing his wits, what do you think? – whether what was readily agreed by everyone, was what *really* happened.

GOVERNESS: What do you want from me?

FLORA: It's obvious, isn't it? I lost both my parents. I had a brother. He and I were in your charge. I wish to know what happened to him.

GOVERNESS: But, Flora, you must remember...

FLORA: Almost nothing. A boy in a brightly coloured waistcoat, no more real than a portrait. A cloudy memory of the very end. A long coach ride I believe. Partial, indistinct. You see, my uncle mentioned your name. It meant nothing to me, and old Mrs Grose has passed away. But then, by chance, my friend Mrs Ashmore was getting rid of her governess. Her children are grown. And there was that name again. Your name. She provided me with your address, and here you are.

GOVERNESS: Mrs Conray –

FLORA: Mrs Conray is my seamstress.

The GOVERNESS is perplexed.

(Continued.) It had to be a name you wouldn't recognise. I'm not married. I have no children. I require no governess. Only the truth. I wish to understand and you shan't leave until I do.

GOVERNESS: Please, Flora, pity me.

FLORA: I don't pretend this little trap is enjoyable – for either of us – but a more formal investigation would inevitably be worse – for you. Strangers – external agencies – would be less accommodating. You see my meaning. For who – what rational outsider – on hearing the facts as I heard them reported, would believe that you should go free?

GOVERNESS: *(Slumping, defeated, into the chair.)* Flora…!

SCENE FIVE.

1840

Bly.

Early summer. Sunlight and mating-season birdsong.

MRS GROSE enters. She's plain, stout, simple and utterly wholesome.

MRS GROSE: Flora! Come here, my love, and help me with these.

FLORA: Yes, Mrs Grose.

38-year-old FLORA has lost 30 years and is now FLORA the child: intelligent, open and charming. She carries a bunch of flowers she's handpicked from the garden.

The GOVERNESS exits.

MRS GROSE: She'll be here any minute.

MRS GROSE and FLORA remove all the remaining dustsheets in readiness for the governess' arrival. MRS GROSE smooths FLORA's hair.

(Continued.) And mind you give the young lady a nice proper curtsey when she arrives. Now, a nice curtsey. That's it.

The GOVERNESS has re-entered with a couple of lightish travelling bags. MRS GROSE and FLORA curtsey deeply.

(Continued.) You're very welcome, miss. *(Taking the bags.)* I hope your journey was pleasant.

GOVERNESS: Oh yes, thank you.

MRS GROSE: The fly gave you no trouble?

GOVERNESS: Not at all – quite commodious. The house and the grounds are so beautiful. The master really did it insufficient justice. And you must be Flora.

FLORA: *(Presenting her flowers.)* I picked these for you.

GOVERNESS: *(Accepting them.)* Aren't they lovely! So pretty. How thoughtful of you. Now let me see, there's marigold and lavender and – Oh! Ah! I think something bit me.

MRS GROSE: Let me see.

The GOVERNESS has been bitten on the inside of her right wrist.

FLORA: It's not poisonous.

MRS GROSE: Oh, now, just a little insect. I'll fetch you some ointment, miss.

GOVERNESS: No no, I'll survive alright!

FLORA laughs.

MRS GROSE: Then Flora will take you to your room –

FLORA: Yes, Mrs Grose –

MRS GROSE: While I see about tea. *(Exits with bags.)*.

FLORA: This way, come along. *(Leading the GOVERNESS about.)* You know, I can sense it. You and I are going to be great friends, aren't we?

GOVERNESS: Yes, Flora, I hope so.

FLORA: Here it is. I'm having my bed moved here beside yours, and when Miles returns from school in a day or two, he'll sleep in that room, the one down the hall. Now, I expect you'd like to see the tower.

GOVERNESS: The tower? Yes, very much.

FLORA: This way. Don't dawdle.

The GOVERNESS is rubbing her right wrist. It itches.

GOVERNESS: Oh what beautiful drapes.

FLORA laughs.

(Continued.) We have nothing like them at home. And that mirror!

FLORA: What's so special about a silly old glass?

GOVERNESS: I've never seen such a thing before.

FLORA: You've never seen yourself from head to foot?

The GOVERNESS is thrilled by her own reflection.

(Continued.) Come, don't you want to climb the tower? It's got machicolated turrets.

GOVERNESS: What are they?

FLORA: For pouring boiling oil out of in the olden days. That's a portrait of my great, great, great grandfather.

GOVERNESS: Ah! His eyes follow you wherever you go. It's uncanny.

FLORA: Miles says it's a visual joke.

GOVERNESS: My word, it's just like 'The Mysteries of Udolpho'!

FLORA: The mysteries of where?

GOVERNESS: One of my favourite books. There's a bit where Emily's been kidnapped and is trapped in the Castle of Udolpho. She explores, just like we're doing now, and comes upon a dusty old portrait with eyes that follow her around. I never thought such a thing could actually exist.

A noise – possibly human but unclear.

(Continued, alarmed.) What was that?

FLORA: What?

GOVERNESS: Shhh. *(They listen.)* It's stopped. I thought I heard… It sounded like a child crying.

FLORA: But you musn't be scared. This house has many strange noises.

MRS GROSE enters with a letter.

(Continued.) And just as many strange people.

MRS GROSE: Time for your tea, my angel.

FLORA: Yes, Mrs Grose.

FLORA exits.

GOVERNESS: Oh, she *is* an angel. Quite like one of Raphael's holy infants. The most beautiful child I've ever seen.

MRS GROSE: If you like the girl, miss, you'll be carried away by the little gentleman.

GOVERNESS: Well, that I think is what I came for – to be carried away. I'm afraid, however, I'm rather easily carried away. I was carried away in London.

MRS GROSE: Ah. Well, you weren't the first.

GOVERNESS: *(Laughing to cover her real feeling.)* I've no pretension to being the only one.

MRS GROSE remembers her letter.

MRS GROSE: This came for you today.

GOVERNESS: *(Glancing at the envelope, thrilled.)* From the master? *(Opens it and reads.)* "This, I recognize, is from the headmaster, and the headmaster's an awful bore. Deal with him, please – but mind you don't report. Not a word. I'm off".

The GOVERNESS breaks open the sealed letter-within-the-letter and scans it. She's shocked.

(Continued.) The child's dismissed his school.

MRS GROSE: But aren't they all sent home?

GOVERNESS: For the holidays. But Miles may never go back at all.

MRS GROSE: *(Tearful.)* Why? What's he done?

The GOVERNESS offers MRS GROSE the letter to read, but MRS GROSE demurs, putting her hands behind her back.

(Continued.) Oh no, miss – such things aren't for me.

GOVERNESS: *(Embarrassed, realising that MRS GROSE probably can't read.)* Oh I see – of course – I'm sorry. Well, there are no particulars, but simply that it's impossible to keep him. It can have only one meaning – that he's an injury to others.

MRS GROSE: *(Affronted.)* Master Miles? An injury? See him first, miss, then believe it. You might as well believe it of the little lady, bless her. Look at her.

FLORA has returned, clutching a doll, and, trying to remain unseen, is staring from a distance at her new governess. The GOVERNESS hasn't noticed but MRS GROSE has.

As soon as the GOVERNESS spies FLORA, she bolts.

GOVERNESS: You've never known the boy to be bad, Mrs Grose?

MRS GROSE: Never? I don't pretend that.

GOVERNESS: Then you have?

MRS GROSE: Yes indeed, miss, thank God.

GOVERNESS: You mean a boy without the spirit to be naughty is no boy for you.

MRS GROSE: Right, miss.

GOVERNESS: But not to the degree to contaminate –

MRS GROSE: Contaminate –?

GOVERNESS: *(Explaining.)* Corrupt.

MRS GROSE: Are you afraid he'll corrupt *you*?

GOVERNESS: No – no such thing! But tell me, what was the lady who was here before?

MRS GROSE: The last governess?

GOVERNESS: I was too nervous to pursue the matter with the master –

MRS GROSE: She was also young and pretty – almost as young and almost as pretty, miss, even as you.

GOVERNESS: He seems to like us young and pretty.

MRS GROSE: Oh, he did. It was the way he liked everyone. *(Catching herself out.)* I mean that's his way – the master's.

GOVERNESS: But who did you speak of first?

MRS GROSE: *(Embarrassed, covering.)* Him, of course.

GOVERNESS: Of the master?

MRS GROSE: *(Deflecting.)* Who else?

GOVERNESS: And my predecessor – did she see anything in the boy that wasn't right?

MRS GROSE: She never told me.

GOVERNESS: Was she careful – particular?

MRS GROSE: *(Guardedly.)* About some things – yes.

GOVERNESS: Not about all?

MRS GROSE: Well, miss – she's gone. I won't tell tales.

GOVERNESS: I understand your feeling. Did she die here?

MRS GROSE: No – she went off.

GOVERNESS: Went off to die?

MRS GROSE looks away.

(Continued, pushing.) She was taken ill, you mean, and went home?

MRS GROSE refuses to engage with the governess.

(Continued, insisting.) Mrs Grose, I believe I have a right to know what a young person engaged in Bly might be –

MRS GROSE: She was not taken ill so far as appeared in this house. She left at the end of the year to go home as she said for a short holiday. But she never came back. At the very moment I was expecting her, I heard from the master that she was dead.

GOVERNESS: But of what?

MRS GROSE: He never told me. But please, miss, I must get to my work.

MRS GROSE exits.

SCENE SIX.

1870

FLORA: An angel, was I? I'd say that was your first mistake, taking me for an angel.

GOVERNESS: You were, oh you were, Flora. Or I was under a spell.

FLORA: I don't believe in spells.

GOVERNESS: Yes, in a storybook – I'd fallen adoze and adream in a romantic castle inhabited by a rosy sprite.

FLORA: Bly's a big, ugly, fairly convenient old house –

GOVERNESS: And we were lost in it! A handful of passengers in a great drifting ship.

FLORA: With you, God help us, at the helm. Twenty years old, with her head in the clouds –

GOVERNESS: *(Rubbing her left wrist, as she invariably does when under pressure.)* God knows, Flora, I did my best. I wanted, no, I fought for what was right for you.

FLORA: What about him?

MILES enters.

GOVERNESS: I don't suppose you could ever understand –

FLORA: Make me then. Explain how you fought for what was right for him.

SCENE SEVEN.

1840

A beaming MRS GROSE follows MILES on.

MRS GROSE: He's come home to us, miss!

MILES, like a charming fairy prince, is as beautiful as FLORA, and even cleverer.

MILES: Here I am. *(Bows to the GOVERNESS.)* You're the new governess, I imagine, come to "do for us", as dear Mrs Grose would say. *(Shakes the governess' hand.).*

GOVERNESS: Delighted to meet you –

MILES: Tremendously nice to meet you. I'm sure we're all going to have a charming time together, *(To MRS GROSE.)* aren't *you*, my dear? *(Takes the GOVERNESS' hand again, inspects her admiringly.)* Oh yes, very pretty. *(Turns her hand and kisses the inside of the right wrist where she was earlier bitten.).* There's a delicious breeze abroad. What do you say to me flying my kite? Oh! *(Hugs the GOVERNESS.)* Very pretty indeed. *(Bounds off.).*

GOVERNESS: *(Turning to MRS GROSE, utterly charmed.)* It's grotesque.

MRS GROSE: What?

GOVERNESS: The cruel charge. It doesn't live an instant. My dear woman, *look* at him.

MRS GROSE: I assure you, miss, I do little else.

GOVERNESS: That great glow of freshness, the same purity his little sister has. What a brute the headmaster must be. How can you feel anything for the boy except a sort of... passion of tenderness? Injury? It's obvious at first sight. He knows nothing but love.

MRS GROSE: What will you say, then?

GOVERNESS: In answer to the letter? Oh… I'm…

MRS GROSE: It's your decision, miss.

GOVERNESS: Yes. Then I've decided. We say nothing.

MRS GROSE: And to his uncle?

GOVERNESS: Nothing.

MRS GROSE: And to the boy himself?

GOVERNESS: Nothing!

MRS GROSE: I'll stand by you. We'll see it out.

GOVERNESS: We'll see it out.

MRS GROSE: *(Greatly relieved.)* Would you mind, miss, if… Oh!

MRS GROSE throws herself at the governess with a rush of emotion and kisses her.

MILES has returned and crept under one of the dustsheets, encouraged by FLORA who again attempts to stay out of sight. She makes the ghoulish sound of a crying child, startling the GOVERNESS, who's even more terrified when MILES, having crept up behind her, taps her on the back, and she turns to see what she thinks for a tiny instant is a ghost. She takes it in good humour.

GOVERNESS: Out, out, the whole pack of you, and let me rest. Mrs Grose – bath and bedtime please.

MILES: *(Sweetly.)* I brought 'Amelia' for you.

GOVERNESS: Oh, where did you –?

MILES: Here.

GOVERNESS: Well, thank you, Miles, what a little treasure you are.

MRS GROSE escorts the children out.

MRS GROSE: Come along you terrors.

The GOVERNESS settles down, making herself properly comfortable in the rocking chair. She chuckles to herself recalling the children's antics, and then starts to read her Henry Fielding. As she begins to enjoy it, she's alerted by a strange noise – a door squeaking or a bird cawing – it's unclear.

She listens carefully…

GOVERNESS: Miles…?

But there's only silence.

She returns to her book, settling into it properly. Stretching, she starts to daydream.

Another noise. Then suddenly, accompanied by a strange but beautiful sound, a man appears to her. It's the EMPLOYER.

The GOVERNESS gasps, is shyly thrilled and incredulous.

Practically as soon as he appears, he disappears again. The blackout exists for a mere moment before lights once more come up, this time accompanied by a terrifying, jarring cacophony. The FIGURE has changed. He's rough, voracious and unrefined, tantalising and threatening, and in much greater physical proximity to the GOVERNESS than the figure of the employer was.

The governess, horrified, screams, and faints.

Blackout.

Act Two

1870

FLORA: *(Attempting to help the governess to her feet.)* Here. Come.

The GOVERNESS, confused, whimpering, pushes FLORA away, retreating – a frightened animal.

(Continued.) It's alright. You fainted.

GOVERNESS: It was…

FLORA: What? What was it?

Again, FLORA goes to help the GOVERNESS rise but she resists, flinching, and pulls away, rubbing her neck with her left wrist.

GOVERNESS: You want to kill me?

FLORA: You saw something? Tell me. No one's here.

GOVERNESS: It. Him. That horror. As clear as he was then…

The GOVERNESS won't move from the floor.

FLORA: My dear, I wish you no harm. I want only to understand. Please, won't you sit? *(Shrugging.)* Very well, let's both sit on the floor.

FLORA joins the GOVERNESS on the floor.

(Continued.) Now then. You're not going to faint again. Nothing can hurt you. *(Puts her arm around the governess.)* You were reading…

GOVERNESS: *(Pleading.)* Flora…

FLORA: You said Miles brought you your book. 'Amelia' – was it? – and you were reading, and there was a noise. You became distracted.

GOVERNESS: *(Massaging her left wrist.)* Distracted? Oh, what a fool I was, a stupid little fool. Like a mooning child, I thought about...

FLORA: About my uncle? Of course you did. You were young, you were full of life...

GOVERNESS: God, I don't suppose he ever thought of me. But I imagined...

FLORA: Naturally – you were romantic.

GOVERNESS: I was ambitious. He'd trusted me with a task, and I was capable of doing it.

Lights change. The GOVERNESS, rising, becomes her youthful self again.

FLORA: You walked out of the house into the grounds.

Sound accompanies us outside.

GOVERNESS: Into the grounds. The June evening gave some little light, and I thought how charming it would be suddenly to meet someone. Someone who would stand before me and smile –

FLORA: And approve...?

GOVERNESS: Only that he should *know*. To see it – the pleasure I gave him by executing my duties so well – the kind light of it in his handsome face. And then...he *did* stand there!

The lights change.

(Continued.) But it wasn't him. It wasn't the master at all *(Becoming breathless, rehearsing her customary twitches.)* It was

no one I knew. Someone predatory, disgusting, terrifying
– the scene, the whole place was stricken, stricken with
death.

FLORA: What do you mean?

GOVERNESS: He never took his eyes from me. Even as he
turned away, he fixed me…

FLORA: And what did you do?

Lights restore, and the GOVERNESS returns to 1870.

GOVERNESS: Nothing.

FLORA: I mean, who did you tell?

GOVERNESS: No one.

FLORA: Not Mrs Grose?

GOVERNESS: I was too frightened.

FLORA: But to say nothing to anyone –

GOVERNESS: Nothing like it happened again for a while. I
came to believe I'd imagined it. There were no mysteries
in Bly. Or it was an intruder, and it was the twilight that
made him seem… And if so, I said to myself, we'd see no
more of him. I threw myself into work. To watch, to teach,
to form you, Flora. And for a while, it was the making of a
happy and useful life for me.

FLORA: And Miles? What did he say about his school – how
he'd come to be expelled?

GOVERNESS: There was… There was something divine in
your brother. Both of you had a gentleness that kept you –
how can I express it? – unpunishable.

FLORA: But he must have said something. What did he admit
to?

GOVERNESS: He was too fine for the unclean school world. He'd paid a price for it, that's all.

FLORA: You mean you didn't ask him.

The GOVERNESS looks at FLORA.

GOVERNESS: And then –

There's a horrifying sound, and lights change to reveal the FIGURE again.

(Continued.) ...he returned!

The GOVERNESS sees it over FLORA's shoulder and screams, recoiling.

A very brief blackout.

MRS GROSE enters with hat and coat. The FIGURE has gone.

MRS GROSE: What in the name of goodness is the matter?

SCENE TWO.

1840

The grounds.

MRS GROSE: You're as white as a sheet.

GOVERNESS: I...I went into the drawing room to pick up my gloves for church and I saw... Outside –

MRS GROSE: What?

GOVERNESS: Outside the window, looking in... A figure.

MRS GROSE: What figure?

GOVERNESS: I don't know. I can't say. Peering in at me. As soon as the first shock subsided, I bolted out of the house to meet him. I ran along the terrace and came full in sight

– but of nothing. The lawn, the garden, the park, they're deserted. He's vanished.

MRS GROSE: Where's he gone?

GOVERNESS: I know still less.

MRS GROSE: Have you seen him before?

GOVERNESS: Yes. Once.

MRS GROSE: And you didn't tell me?

GOVERNESS: No. I was…

MRS GROSE: Was he a gentleman?

GOVERNESS: No. No.

MRS GROSE: Nobody from the village?

GOVERNESS: I made sure.

MRS GROSE: But if he isn't a gentleman –?

GOVERNESS: He's a horror. God help me if I know *what* he is.

MRS GROSE: *(Offering the coat.)* It's time we should be at church.

GOVERNESS: Oh, I'm not fit for church.

MRS GROSE: Won't it do you good?

GOVERNESS: It won't do them any good.

MRS GROSE: The children?

GOVERNESS: I can't leave them. *(Pause.)*. You go to church. I must watch.

MRS GROSE: I don't believe I could have followed him out.

GOVERNESS: *(Laughs.)* Neither could I. But I *did.* I have my duty.

MRS GROSE: *(Offended.)* So have I mine. What was he like?

GOVERNESS: Like nobody I've… A long, pale face, with straight, good features. Eyebrows darker than his hair, eyes sharp, clean-shaven, without a hat. Tall, active, alive. Never, no never a gentleman.

MRS GROSE: A gentleman? A gentleman – *he?*

GOVERNESS: You know him?

MRS GROSE: He *is* handsome?

GOVERNESS: Remarkably.

MRS GROSE: And dressed…?

GOVERNESS: In somebody else's clothes. They're smart, but I'm sure they're not his.

MRS GROSE: They're the master's!

GOVERNESS: No, I tell you, it's not the master! At first I thought it was, but –

MRS GROSE: It's Quint.

GOVERNESS: Quint?

MRS GROSE: Peter Quint – the master's own man, his valet when he was here. He never wore his hat, but he did wear – well, there were waistcoats missed. The master believed in him and placed him here because he was supposed not to be well and the country air good for him. Then the master went, and Quint was alone.

GOVERNESS: Alone?

MRS GROSE: Alone with *us.* In charge, with everything to say.

GOVERNESS: And what became of him?

MRS GROSE: He went, too.

GOVERNESS: Went where?

MRS GROSE: God knows where. He died.

GOVERNESS: Died?

MRS GROSE: Yes. Mr Quint is dead.

SCENE THREE.

1870

FLORA: She saw nothing.

GOVERNESS: She identified Quint from my description.

FLORA: But she *saw* nothing. Not the shadow of a shadow.

GOVERNESS: Not then, perhaps, but she believed that I saw.

FLORA: That you saw a ghost.

GOVERNESS: Yes, yes! She accepted what I told her. She was my counsellor.

MRS GROSE enters.

(Continued.) She was tender and kind. Far more than her position obliged her to be.

SCENE FOUR.

1840

Later the same night.

The GOVERNESS paces thoughtfully.

MRS GROSE: He was peeping, was he? Peering at you through the drawing room window.

GOVERNESS: Yes, our eyes met. I turned cold. It was as if I'd been looking at him for years and had known him always. But this time, something was different.

MRS GROSE: How?

GOVERNESS: Because, through the glass, though he gazed into my face as deep and hard as before, presently his eyes left me and fixed on other things. It came to me in an instant – this time he came for someone else. This time he came for Miles.

MRS GROSE: Little Miles? How do you know?

GOVERNESS: I know! I feel it! And you do too, my dear!

MRS GROSE is appalled.

(Continued.) But it's so curious. Why has neither child ever mentioned Quint having been here – the time they were with him – even his name?

MRS GROSE: Oh, I don't think the little lady would remember. She never knew how he died.

GOVERNESS: How did he die?

MRS GROSE: Well, they found him on the road one morning with a wound to his head – one of the labourers did. It was wintertime, the paths were icy. *(Mimes drinking.)* They said

29

he took a wrong turning from the pub. Well, there were plenty of people who were happy to see him gone.

GOVERNESS: Miles would have remembered that.

MRS GROSE: Ah, don't try him.

GOVERNESS: Why be afraid? Still, it's very odd.

MRS GROSE: That Miles never spoke of his friend, you mean?

GOVERNESS: His 'friend'?

MRS GROSE: No, well, it was Quint's own fancy. To play with him, I mean. To spoil him. Quint was much too free.

GOVERNESS: Too free with my boy?

MRS GROSE: Too free with everyone.

GOVERNESS: Quint was definitely bad then?

MRS GROSE: Well, I knew it – but the master couldn't see it.

GOVERNESS: Why didn't you tell him?

MRS GROSE: He hated tale bearing. If people were all right to him, he didn't bother with more.

GOVERNESS: I would have told him.

MRS GROSE: Really? Can you be sure?

GOVERNESS: As far as sheltering the children is concerned, when I ran out to find Quint in the grounds today, I discovered what I'm capable of.

MRS GROSE: *(Abashed.)* I dare say I was wrong. But, really, I was afraid.

GOVERNESS: Of what?

MRS GROSE: The things that man could do. He was so clever – he was so deep.

GOVERNESS: You weren't afraid of anything else? Not of his effect –?

MRS GROSE: *(Anguished.)* His effect?

GOVERNESS: On innocent precious little lives, who were in *your charge*!

SCENE FIVE.

1870

FLORA: But now we were in *your* charge. After what you'd witnessed, why didn't you contact our uncle to request that he remove me and Miles from the house?

GOVERNESS: I told you, it was forbidden to contact him about anything.

FLORA: Not in a case like this, for God's sake.

GOVERNESS: That was the contractual reason. The occasion demanded heroism from me, and I was determined –

FLORA: Ah, the wellspring of your delusion! If your heroism could be seen in the right quarter – in Weymouth Street – you might succeed romantically where many another girl had failed.

GOVERNESS: *(Rubbing her left wrist.)* I wasn't acting for me. I had a service to perform – to defend you. The decision was simple. If the apparition appeared again, I'd offer myself to it.

FLORA: *(After a moment of shock.)* Meaning?

GOVERNESS: I'd be a fence around you to save you. My heart ached to save you. We were cut off, Flora – united in our danger. You'd nothing but me, and I – well, I had *you*. How could work not be charming that presented itself

31

as daily beauty? For a long time, I was dazzled by your loveliness. With your voices in the air and your fragrant faces against my cheek, everything fell to the ground but your incapacity and your beauty. But then there came the moment when I began to think your charms might be entirely studied.

FLORA: I beg your pardon?

GOVERNESS: I discerned in you a knowledge…

FLORA: Of what?

GOVERNESS: Why dissemble, Flora? You remember. You knew what I saw. You knew it yourself exactly. You knew it then – you *must* know it now.

FLORA: That's a nonsensical assertion. What did I know?

GOVERNESS: The day we spent by the lake – you recall. You made a boat. Surely you can't have forgotten what happened to us by the lake.

FLORA: I made a boat? Unlikely. Out of what?

GOVERNESS: Out of old scraps of wood – and ingenuity!

SCENE SIX.

1840/1870

Lights lead us outdoors. High summer. Birdsong.

GOVERNESS: Look, Flora. There's a scrap of something might be useful for you.

FLORA: *(Picking something off the ground.)* Oh, it's the perfect shape for a rudder. Now all I need is something to do for the mast. *(Hunts about.).*

GOVERNESS: That day I was, oh, I can't recall – some remarkable person that your game required. And, because we'd lately begun geography, the lake was the Sea of Azov. I was certainly something that could sit, because I'd sat down with a piece of work...

She's picked up some embroidery and sat, keeping her eyes on her work.

Lights have begun to dim. Sounds darken and vibrate.

(Continued.) ...when, out of nowhere, I became aware, on the other side of the lake...

A WOMAN appears in a black dress. With her haggard beauty and her unutterable woe, she is as dark as midnight [– and played by the male actor].

(Continued.) ...another presence... Fixing my eyes on my work, I counted possibilities. It had to be the gardener or a messenger or a tradesman's boy from the village. Nothing was more natural...

The GOVERNESS finally turns to look at the WOMAN. The WOMAN looks at FLORA, with great intensity. Sound peaks.

(Continued.) ...But it was no such natural thing. It was an alien object. A hideous thing. Did you see it too? You'd turned your back to the water...

FLORA has turned her back to the stranger.

(Continued.) You'd found yourself a mast and you were attempting to tighten it in place...

FLORA is doing so.

(Continued.) You were screwing in the mast, screwing and screwing, so intently, brazenly yes, violently. And I knew in that moment that you knew too. You knew.

The figure in the black dress disappears.

SCENE SEVEN.

1840

GOVERNESS: *(Almost hysterical, pacing agitatedly.)* It's too monstrous. They *know*.

MRS GROSE: *(Alarmed.)* What? What on earth do they know?

GOVERNESS: All that *we* know – and heaven knows what else besides. Flora *saw*.

MRS GROSE: *(Almost winded by the news.)* She told you?

GOVERNESS: Not a word – that's the horror. She kept it to herself. A child of eight, *that* child.

MRS GROSE: Didn't you challenge her?

GOVERNESS: And risk losing her forever?

MRS GROSE: Then how do you know?

GOVERNESS: I saw with my eyes that she was perfectly aware.

MRS GROSE: Do you mean aware of *him*?

GOVERNESS: Of *her*. A woman in black – pale and dreadful – with such an air, and such a face. A horror of horrors.

MRS GROSE: Someone you've never seen before?

GOVERNESS: Someone the child has. Someone *you* have. My predecessor. The governess who died.

MRS GROSE: Miss Jessel?

GOVERNESS: Miss Jessel.

MRS GROSE: *(Distressed.)* But how can you be sure?

GOVERNESS: Ask Flora – *she's* sure. No, for God's sake, *don't*. She'll say she isn't – she'll lie.

34

MRS GROSE: Ah, how *can* you?

GOVERNESS: Because she doesn't want me to know. There are depths. The more I go over it, the more I see in it, and the more I see in it, the more I fear.

MRS GROSE: Fear seeing her again?

GOVERNESS: Fear not seeing her.

MRS GROSE: Oh! I don't understand you.

GOVERNESS: I'm frightened the child may keep it up – and she assuredly will – without my knowing it.

MRS GROSE: Dear dear – we must keep our heads. Tell me how you know she was Miss Jessel.

GOVERNESS: Then you admit it's what she was?

MRS GROSE: Tell me how you know.

GOVERNESS: By seeing her. By the way she looked.

MRS GROSE: At you, you mean? So wickedly?

GOVERNESS: She gave me never a glance. She only fixed the child.

MRS GROSE: Fixed her?

GOVERNESS: With such awful eyes.

MRS GROSE: Do you mean of dislike?

GOVERNESS: Of something much worse. With a determination – indescribable. With a kind of fury of intention.

MRS GROSE: Tention?

GOVERNESS: To get hold of her.

MRS GROSE shudders and walks a few steps away.

(Continued.) That's what Flora *knows*.

MRS GROSE: The person was in black?

GOVERNESS: In mourning – rather poor, almost shabby. But – yes – with extraordinary beauty.

MRS GROSE is coming to believe.

(Continued.) Wonderfully handsome, but infamous.

MRS GROSE: Miss Jessel – *was* infamous. They were both infamous.

GOVERNESS: I must have it now, my dear. Of what did she die?

MRS GROSE hesitates.

On a separate part of the stage, lights reveal MILES and FLORA. They're outside playing on the lawn, messing about – rolling over each other. Is it simply a gleeful childish game, or possibly something more sinister? It could look like the children are recreating, mirthfully, unaware of the implications, Quint and Jessel rolling over each other in the throws of sexual abandon.

(Continued.) Come, there was something between them.

MRS GROSE: There was everything.

GOVERNESS: In spite of the difference of their rank? You said she was a lady –

MRS GROSE: And he so dreadfully below.

GOVERNESS: The fellow was a hound.

MRS GROSE: I've never seen one like him. He did what he wished.

GOVERNESS: With her?

MRS GROSE: With them all.

GOVERNESS: So, he was impudent and assured and spoiled and... depraved. But for all his evil, it must have been also what *she* wished.

MRS GROSE: And poor woman – she paid for it.

GOVERNESS: You *do* know what she died of.

MRS GROSE: I know nothing. I was glad enough I didn't, and I thanked heaven she was well out of this.

GOVERNESS: Yet you had your idea of her real reason for leaving.

MRS GROSE: As to that, she couldn't have stayed. Fancy it here – for a governess... *(Subtly mimes pregnancy.)*. And afterward I imagined – and I still imagine. And what I imagine is dreadful.

GOVERNESS: And what I imagine is worse. There's a particularly deadly view I'm finding it hard to deny – a direction in which I may not for the present let myself go. *(Desperate.)* Oh God, I don't do it. I don't save or shield them. It's as bad as I feared – they're lost.

Blackout.

INTERVAL.

Act Three

The sky is grey and the space bare. Dead leaves are scattered around the stage, like a theatre after the performance, strewn with crumpled cast lists.

SCENE ONE.

1840

As in Act One, with house lights dimming, sound takes us to a sketchier, scarier place. Blackness envelopes the auditorium and the sound of a music box distorts eerily. A fluttering of birds' wings suggests panic and chaos, and then a whistling wind whips up. QUINT is suddenly, indistinctly before us, bearing a candle that produces a small amount of warm dusty light. We can barely make him out. He raises the flame to his face, his features becoming clearer with every inch, and, as he extinguishes the light, we're plunged back into darkness and the wind rises fantastically to blot everything else out.

As quickly as possible, lights are restored, the wind has died away, QUINT has gone, the GOVERNESS reads her book and MRS GROSE has entered with a tea tray. She pours for two as middle-aged FLORA enters.

SCENE TWO.

1870

FLORA: Life was normal. Happy in Bly. Except that Miles and I stood in moral and mortal danger. At any moment, the depraved Quint or this Miss Jessel might –

GOVERNESS: 'This Miss Jessel'? What? You think I make her up? Invent a danger where none existed? I gave a picture disclosing to the last detail the special marks of both phantoms, and Mrs Grose's response was instantly to recognize and name them.

FLORA: Certainly. You were her superior – she knew her place.

The GOVERNESS is incredulous, her nervous spasms returning.

(Continued.) Mrs Grose felt the need to please you! Her employment depended on it, and you were determined to bend her to your will. If you wished to mix a witch's broth and proposed it confidently, she'd have held out a large clean saucepan. Perhaps she also read 'Clarissa' and 'Amelia'.

GOVERNESS: I told you – she couldn't read.

FLORA: The first time you saw Quint, you'd put your book down, wandered into the garden fantasising about seeing my uncle, and come face to face with the kind of dashing evil villain you read about in your books. Those heartless, hatless, devilishly good-looking scoundrels!

GOVERNESS: You had communion with the ghost of Miss Jessel! I witnessed it! And I saw that it was a matter of habit – for both of you!

FLORA: You saw that, did you?

GOVERNESS: How you'd fought with those little bits of wood, to show me you hadn't seen. You wanted, by just so much as you did see, to make me suppose you didn't.

FLORA: The fact that I didn't see proved that I did? The witch is guilty either way. I was making a boat, not on the look out for ghosts. From my screwing something into a hole, you imagine I was in league with malign shadows? I was an angel who schemed with spectres. I was pure innocence and guilty as hell.

GOVERNESS: There were contradictions everywhere! You must understand – clues came only one by one. It was only through countless sleepless nights that I reached any answers at all. My God, Flora, I hardly *wished* to see evil – least of all in you. I'd gaze into the depths of your blue eyes, and see how impossible it was to think their loveliness a trick of deceit or cunning.

FLORA: But you don't have proof. Real proof.

GOVERNESS: Oh, real proof came later.

FLORA: Then why don't I remember something of it?

GOVERNESS: You do. But you've forced yourself to forget because it's too painful to hold on to.

MRS GROSE hands the governess a cup of tea.

SCENE THREE.

1840, and a flashback to an even earlier time. MILES enters.

MRS GROSE: *(Drinking tea.)* And I can't pretend they weren't together all the time for months. And I, well, I didn't think it right, not at all. Miss Jessel was their governess. But Miles kept to Quint day-in and day-out, and the little lady all the time with Miss Jessel. I even went so far as to talk frankly to her about it.

GOVERNESS: To Miss Jessel?

MRS GROSE: And, well, she told me, in no uncertain terms, to mind my own business.

GOVERNESS: You talked to the boy himself?

MRS GROSE: I did. I said *(To MILES.)* I hope you won't take it amiss, master Miles, but I like to see a young gentleman remember his station.

MILES: *(On his rocking horse.)* Remember my station? What on earth does that mean?

GOVERNESS: *(To MRS GROSE.)* You reminded him that Quint was only a base menial?

MRS GROSE: Indeed I did. *(To MILES.)* You know very well. It's not right for the young master of the house to spend so much time with an under-stairs man.

GOVERNESS: And what was his answer?

MRS GROSE: Bad.

MILES: Why shouldn't I spend time with the fellow, my dear? Peter's my friend. After all, who I choose to call friend is not your responsibility.

MRS GROSE: But the man goes about with you quite as if he's your tutor – and a very grand one –

MILES: You won't make false accusations like that. How do you know where I go and what I do? I won't have it.

GOVERNESS: He lied!

MILES: And if you don't like me spending time with base menials, Mrs Grose, then I shouldn't be talking to *you*, for you're just another. *(Dismounts the horse and exits.)*.

GOVERNESS: He said that? *(MRS GROSE nods.)*. And you forgave him?

MRS GROSE: Well, wouldn't *you*?

GOVERNESS: Yes.

The women laugh ruefully, united in their mutual inferiority to Master MILES.

(Continued.) What those villains succeeded in making of him. He knew, I suppose, what went on between them?

MRS GROSE: I don't know. *(Starts collecting tea things together.)*.

GOVERNESS: Yes you do. Only you haven't my dreadful boldness of mind to say it.

MRS GROSE: Well, there's nothing in him that's not nice now.

GOVERNESS: Indeed – he's a prodigy of lovable goodness, *now*.

The moon has risen. MILES and FLORA run on. He lights a candle. She's dressed as a fairy and carries a music box.

Well, I shall watch them harder from now. And I intend never to be out of their company.

The GOVERNESS is dragged, book in hand, into the schoolroom by the children. MRS GROSE exits with tea things.

SCENE FOUR.

1840

The schoolroom.

MILES: You will permit us to perform the scene we've learned for you, won't you?

GOVERNESS: Miles, I was reading.

MILES: Oh, boring.

FLORA: Please please let us. We've rehearsed it 'specially for you.

MILES: I've directed it and *(producing a horse head mask.)* made the props and everything.

GOVERNESS: I wonder sometimes whether you're really a child at all, dear Miles.

MILES: Say yes.

GOVERNESS: Yes!

FLORA squeaks in triumph, and sets the music box to play.

MILES: *(Directing the governess.)* Right, you must sit there. This will be the stage, you see? Now *(Putting on his horse mask.)* I play Bottom.

FLORA: And I play Titania. *(Lies down.).*

GOVERNESS: Oh, brava, Flora.

FLORA: Shh, I'm asleep. *(Sleeps.).*

MILES: *(As Bottom, holding the lit candle.)* 'Why do they run away? This is to make an ass of me, to fright me, if they could. But I will walk up and down, and I will sing, that they shall hear I'm not afraid'. *(Sings.)*

FLORA: *(Waking up.)* 'What angel wakes me from my flowery bed?'

MILES/BOTTOM is startled and stops singing.

(Continued.) 'I pray thee, gentle mortal, sing again. Mine ear is much enamour'd of thy note. So is mine eye enthrallèd to thy shape. And thy fair virtue's force perforce doth move me to swear I love thee'.

MILES: 'Methinks, you should have little reason for that, and yet, to say the truth, reason and love keep little company together nowadays'.

FLORA: 'Thou art as wise as thou art beautiful'.

MILES: 'Not so. But if I had wit enough to get out of this wood –'

FLORA: 'Therefore, go with me. / I'll give thee fairies to attend on thee / and I will purge thy mortal grossness so / that thou shalt like an airy spirit go'.

MILES and FLORA exit dramatically together. The GOVERNESS, delighted, applauds. She waits for the children to come back 'on' for a curtain call, but they don't. Initially she's amused, assuming a little trick is being played.

GOVERNESS: I see. Highly amusing. I see their knavery! 'This is to make an ass of me, to fright me' indeed! Children?

She becomes concerned. Lights change subtly – becoming dimmer and more shadowy. The GOVERNESS picks up MILES' candle to investigate, but can see neither child. The music box, having been bright and cheerful, sounds discordant.

(Continued.) Flora? Miles? Mrs Grose? *(Scared.)* Alright, that's enough.

A sharp but unidentifiable noise – like someone far off screaming. The GOVERNESS gasps.

(Continued.) Come. I command you…

There's another sudden jagged pulse of sound and QUINT appears. She immediately senses him and turns to face him.

SCENE FIVE

Carrying his own candle, QUINT approaches her until he is close. She is terrified and remains rooted to the spot. This time, there's nothing ghostly about him. Instead he's a living, detestable, dangerous presence.

Neither of them move. There's an intensity between them which could go any way and the provocation is not entirely on his side. There's a sexual element to it.

Terror recedes, but not intensity. For a moment, it looks as if she will move towards him, even somehow offer herself to him. Their bodies seem drawn together. Something breaks. He withdraws. She has, at least, outfaced him. He slinks off. His candle is extinguished. He's gone.

She breathes again, conflicted and overwhelmed. She retraces the steps to her bedroom with the only light her candle. She believes herself to be home and dry until there's a voice from a source too dimly lit to identify, at least at first.

FLORA: *(A spine-chilling voice, not of a child.)* You naughty! Where *have* you been?

GOVERNESS: *(Shocked, then spotting FLORA, angry.)* Why do you hide in the shadows?

FLORA: *(Normal, sweet voice again.)* Because I don't like to frighten you.

GOVERNESS: Then why did you use that odd voice?

FLORA: What voice?

GOVERNESS: What are you doing with the window open?

FLORA: Looking for you, you dear.

GOVERNESS: Out of the window? You thought I might be walking in the grounds in the middle of the night?

FLORA: Well, you know, I thought someone was.

GOVERNESS: And do you see anyone?

FLORA: *(In a childish whine.)* Ah, *no...*

GOVERNESS: Why are you lying to me? Come away from the window.

FLORA doesn't move. The GOVERNESS grips her arm to pull her away.

(Continued.) There's a figure out there, isn't there? Isn't there? Prowling. Is it...a person you know?

FLORA: Look for yourself.

The GOVERNESS looks, and sees...

GOVERNESS: There *is* someone there! *(Astounded.)* Ah! It's Miles!

FLORA: Who did you expect?

GOVERNESS: And at such a monstrous hour.

The GOVERNESS strides off.

FLORA: Where are you going?

GOVERNESS: To bring him in of course.

SCENE SIX

The GOVERNESS hauls MILES by the arm, marching him to his bedroom.

GOVERNESS: *(Controlling her fear and her temper, with her hands on MILES' shoulders.)* You must tell me – and the truth. What did you go out for? What were you doing down there?

MILES: *(Smiling.)* If I tell you why I did it, will you understand?

The GOVERNESS nods.

(Continued.) Just exactly in order that you should do this.

GOVERNESS: Do what?

MILES: Think me – for a change *(Sweetly and gaily.)* bad!

MILES kisses the GOVERNESS – bright and chaste – and she kisses him back, then embraces him. She has difficulty not crying.

GOVERNESS: You didn't undress at all?

MILES: Not at all. I sat up and read.

GOVERNESS: And when did you go down?

MILES: At midnight. When I'm bad, I *am* bad.

GOVERNESS: *(Trying to put a brave face on it.)* I see, I see – it's charming. But how could you be sure I'd know it?

MILES: I arranged it with Flora. She was to look out.

GOVERNESS: Which is what she did do.

MILES: And to see what she was looking at, you also looked – you saw.

GOVERNESS: While you caught your death in the night air.

MILES: How otherwise should I have been bad enough?

They embrace again.

(Continued.) But just think, you know, *(Tantalisingly.)* what I *might* do!

SCENE SEVEN

GOVERNESS: He knows down to the ground what he *might* do. He thinks he can act however he likes with all his cleverness to help him, but he can't play at innocence any longer. The moon was bright enough for me to see everything. He was gazing at something, as if fascinated. It was Quint. Or perhaps Quint and Jessel too. Depend on it – the four of them perpetually meet. If you'd been with either child tonight, you'd have understood. They pretend to be lost in a fairytale of music and love and private theatricals, but they're steeped in a vision of the dead restored. When they're alone, they're talking of *them*. I know – I go on as if I were crazy. It's a wonder I'm not. What I've seen would have made *you* so. But it's only made me lucid, made me get hold of another thing.

MRS GROSE: *(Sewing.)* What other thing have you got hold of?

GOVERNESS: Of the thing that's delighted me, and yet mystified and troubled me. Their more than earthly beauty. Their unnatural goodness. It's a game. A fraud.

MRS GROSE: On the part of the little darlings?

GOVERNESS: Mad as that seems. They haven't been good – they've only been absent.

MRS GROSE: What, like ghosts, you mean?

GOVERNESS: It's easy to live with them because they lead a life of their own. They're not mine – they're not ours. They're his and they're hers.

MRS GROSE: Quint's and that woman's?

GOVERNESS: Those devils want to get to them for the love of all the evil that, in those dreadful days, the pair put into them, and to ply them with more – to keep up the work of demons. That's what brings them back.

MRS GROSE: Laws! They *were* rascals, but what can they really do to the children?

GOVERNESS: Do? They can destroy them. They've just to keep to their suggestions of danger –

MRS GROSE: For the children to come –?

GOVERNESS: And perish in the attempt! Unless we can prevent it.

MRS GROSE: Their uncle must do the preventing.

GOVERNESS: What?

MRS GROSE: He must take them away.

GOVERNESS: But who's to make him?

MRS GROSE: You, miss.

GOVERNESS: By writing to him that his house is poisoned and his nephew and niece mad?

MRS GROSE: But if they *are*, miss?

GOVERNESS: Charming news to be sent by a governess whose prime undertaking was to give him no worry.

MRS GROSE: But he ought to be here – he ought to help.

GOVERNESS: Can you honestly see me asking him for a visit? *(Frightened.)* If you should lose your head and appeal to him –

MRS GROSE: *(Equally frightened.)* Yes, miss?

GOVERNESS: I'd leave both him and you on the spot.

SCENE EIGHT

1870

FLORA: Said with all the petulance of a cornered adolescent. You couldn't face the ugliness and the pain of it – risk his amusement at your failure – his contempt – risk attracting his attention to your slighted charms. Surely Mrs Grose must have written anyway, despite your threat?

GOVERNESS: Mrs Grose could write no more than she could read.

FLORA: Miles then. He must have wished to know why he wasn't enrolled in another school now autumn had come. Even I? Didn't I reply to his letters?

GOVERNESS: He never sent you letters.

FLORA: Really? It's hard to fathom the depths of my uncle's indifference.

GOVERNESS: What need had he? He trusted me.

FLORA: But weren't we curious about him?

GOVERNESS: Naturally, and you both wrote regularly. But your letters were far too beautiful to post. I kept them myself. I have them to this day.

FLORA: Good God.

GOVERNESS: You understood they were no more than a literary exercise.

FLORA: Did we?

GOVERNESS: You understood everything.

FLORA: Really?

GOVERNESS: Your awareness of what was happening was the air in which we moved. There were occasions when almost every conversation skirted forbidden ground.

FLORA: By that you mean 'the others', the 'dead returning' –

GOVERNESS: I mean your friendship with them! Even in the schoolroom, there were times when they visited you and you welcomed them – and I was ready to shout "They're here, you little wretches, they're here. You can't deny it now", because whatever I saw, you two saw more.

SCENE NINE

1840

A bright, sharp Sunday morning. Church bells merrily chime.

MRS GROSE and MILES are both dressed for church in coats and hats. She hands a coat to FLORA and escorts her off. MILES offers the GOVERNESS her coat.

MILES: *(Charmingly.)* Look here, my dear, you know, when in the world, please, am I going back to school?

The GOVERNESS is lost for words.

(Continued.) You know that for a fellow to be with a lady *always* –

GOVERNESS: And always with the *same* lady?

MILES: Can feel somewhat smothering at times.

GOVERNESS: I smother you? Is that what you're saying?

MILES: Of course, she's a jolly 'perfect' lady, but after all I'm a fellow – don't you see – who's, well, getting on.

GOVERNESS: *(Struggling for composure.)* Yes, you're getting on.

MILES: You know what a boy wants. And you can't say I've not been awfully good, can you?

GOVERNESS: No, I can't say that, Miles.

MILES: Except just that one night, you know, when I went down – out of the house.

GOVERNESS: Oh, yes. *(Fishing.)* But I forget what you did it for.

MILES: *(Reproachfully.)* You forget? It was to show you I could. And I can again.

GOVERNESS: Certainly. But you won't.

MILES: Not *that* again. It was nothing.

GOVERNESS: We must catch the others up.

MILES: *(Delaying.)* Then when *am* I going back?

GOVERNESS: Were you very happy at school?

MILES: I'm happy enough anywhere.

GOVERNESS: Well, if you're just as happy here –

MILES: Ah, but being happy isn't everything. Of course, you know a lot –

GOVERNESS: You mean you know almost as much.

MILES: Not half I want to. Anyway, it isn't so much that, either.

GOVERNESS: What is it, then? That I 'smother you'.

MILES: I want to see more life. I want my own sort.

GOVERNESS: *(Laughing.)* There aren't many of your own sort, Miles. Unless perhaps dear little Flora –

MILES: You compare me to a baby girl?

GOVERNESS: Don't you love our sweet Flora then?

MILES: If I didn't – and you too… Oh, if I didn't…

GOVERNESS: Yes?

MILES: Well, you know what.

GOVERNESS: You'd make a sudden strike for freedom? You're a boy. A very grand one. What could I do?

MILES: Does my uncle think what *you* think?

GOVERNESS: How do you know what I think?

MILES: Well I don't – for you never tell me. But I mean, does he know?

GOVERNESS: Know what, Miles?

MILES: The way I'm going on.

GOVERNESS: I don't think your uncle much cares.

MILES: You think he can't be made to?

GOVERNESS: How?

MILES: Well, by coming down of course.

GOVERNESS: But who'll get him to come down?

MILES: *I* will.

MILES bounds off in the direction MRS GROSE took FLORA to church.

SCENE TEN

1870/1840

Underscore: a hymn from the church service thirty years before.

FLORA: He was absolutely right: Either clear up with my
uncle the mystery of this interruption of my studies, or
cease to expect me to lead with you a life that's unnatural
for a boy.

GOVERNESS: Quite. But Miles was far too clever for even a
bad governess or, let's say, a mere parson's daughter to
spoil.

FLORA: The boy needed proper schooling!

GOVERNESS: He was clever enough without it.

FLORA: Nonsense. And why keep him at Bly to contaminate
and corrupt?

GOVERNESS: In hindsight, it's obvious what was happening,
I grant you. His child's brain was under the influence of a
much older one. *(Massaging her left wrist.)* And the minute
Miles ran from me, I was desperate to flee from him – for
the first time since I saw him, I wanted to get away from
him, from all of you.

FLORA: Oh, if only you had.

GOVERNESS: No one would have blamed me for giving the
whole thing up. And by the time I reached the empty

53

house I'd made up my mind to it. I'd fly. I made for the
schoolroom to collect my belongings, and –

*The hymn has faded out. Lights and sound change. MISS JESSEL
appears. The GOVERNESS is rooted to the spot.*

MISS JESSEL rocks herself in the rocking chair.

(Continued.) There in clear noonday light: my vile
predecessor – your old friend Miss Jessel.

FLORA: *(Witheringly.)* My old friend…

GOVERNESS: Gazing at me as if to say her right to sit in my
chair was as good as mine to sit in hers. For a moment
I felt that *I* was the intruder, and I spoke only to assert
myself as the living creature. *(To MISS JESSEL.)* You
terrible, miserable woman…

*MISS JESSEL seems to hear. With a grand melancholy of indifference,
she rises and leaves. Sound and lights restore. The GOVERNESS
stills the chair.*

(Continued.) And the next minute, there was nothing in the
room but the sunshine, and a new conviction that I would
have to stay. *(Slumps into the chair.).*

FLORA: "You terrible miserable woman". Is that what you
said? Who were you talking to?

SCENE ELEVEN

1840

MRS GROSE: *(Taking her coat off.)* Why didn't you come to
church?

GOVERNESS: I had to meet a friend.

MRS GROSE: A friend?!

GOVERNESS: *(Laughing.)* Yes, I have a couple! It's all out now, between Miles and me.

MRS GROSE: All? But what?

GOVERNESS: Everything. It doesn't matter. I've made up my mind. I had a talk with Miss Jessel.

MRS GROSE: You mean she spoke?

GOVERNESS: It came to that. I found her, on my return, in the schoolroom.

MRS GROSE: And what did she say?

GOVERNESS: That she suffers the torments.

MRS GROSE: You mean…of the lost?

GOVERNESS: Of the lost. Of the damned.

MRS GROSE: So you've made up your mind – to what?

GOVERNESS: To everything.

MRS GROSE: What do you call 'everything'?

GOVERNESS: Sending for their uncle of course.

MRS GROSE: Oh, miss, in pity do.

GOVERNESS: I will. It's the only way. Miles wants more freedom and intends to exploit my fears to get it. Well, if he thinks I'm too frightened to write a letter, he's mistaken. If the master wants to know why I've done nothing about Miles' schooling, I'll put it to him that I can't undertake to resolve the issue of a child who's been expelled –

MRS GROSE: For we've never in-the-least known what.

GOVERNESS: For wickedness. What else, when he's so clever and beautiful and perfect? Is he stupid? Untidy? Ill-natured? He's exquisite. It can be only wickedness. That'll open the whole thing up. After all, it's the master's own fault if he left people like Quint here to educate the boy in depravity. I'll write tonight.

SCENE TWELVE

The sound of rain lashing and powerful gusts battering at the windows.

The GOVERNESS gathers up a candle to write a letter, and sits. On another part of the stage, MILES, in his room, gets into bed with a book.

After writing a few words, the GOVERNESS, alerted by a noise, takes up her candle, and creeps along the corridor to listen, as if at MILES' door.

MILES: *(Gaily.)* I say – you there – come in!

Realising the game is up, the GOVERNESS steps forward, into MILES' room.

GOVERNESS: How did you know I was there?

MILES: *(Laughing.)* You fancy you made no noise? You're like a troop of cavalry marching up and down the hallways, listening at doors.

GOVERNESS: *(Setting down the candle.)* Then you weren't asleep?

MILES: Not much. I lie awake and think.

MILES holds out his hand, which the governess takes.

GOVERNESS: *(Perching on the edge of his bed.)* What is it that you think of?

MILES: What in the world, my dear, but *you*?

GOVERNESS: I'm delighted, but I had so much rather you slept.

MILES: Well, you know, I think also of this queer business of ours, and all the rest.

GOVERNESS: What do you mean, 'all the rest'?

MILES: Oh, you know…

The wind howls.

GOVERNESS: *(Maintaining eye contact.)* Certainly you shall go back to school if you wish. Not to the old place – we must find a better. How could I know you were dissatisfied, when you never spoke of it?

MILES smiles and looks around – for an escape route or inspiration?

(Continued.) Why do you hesitate? Where do you look? Are you hoping for help from someone?

The rain whips against the window.

(Continued.) You know, you've never said a word to me about your old school.

MILES: Haven't I?

GOVERNESS: Not about your masters, your comrades, nor the least little thing that ever happened. Till this morning, you've scarce even made a reference to anything in your previous life, so naturally I thought you were content to go on as you are.

MILES: *(With a languid shake of his head.)* I'm not. I want to go.

GOVERNESS: You want to go to your uncle?

MILES: Ah, you can't get away with that.

GOVERNESS: My dear, I don't want to get away with anything.

MILES: You can't – even if you do, you can't. My uncle must come down and you must completely settle things.

GOVERNESS: If he comes, you may be sure it will be to take you quite away.

MILES: Well, that's exactly what I'm working for. You'll have to tell him about the way you've let it all drop – you'll have to tell him a tremendous lot.

GOVERNESS: And how much will *you* have to tell him? There are things he'll ask you.

MILES: Very likely. But what things?

GOVERNESS: Things you've never told me. To make up his mind what to do with you.

MILES: I want a new field.

GOVERNESS: *(Embracing him.)* Dear little Miles!

Their faces are close. She kisses him. He seems to accept it with good humour.

MILES: Well, old lady?

GOVERNESS: Is there nothing – nothing at all you want to tell me?

MILES: *(Turning away.)* I've told you. I told you this morning. To let me alone.

She lets go his hand, rises from the bed, but stays close.

GOVERNESS: I've just begun a letter to your uncle.

MILES: Well, finish it then!

Pause.

GOVERNESS: *(Reckless, desperate.)* What happened before, Miles?

58

MILES: Before what?

GOVERNESS: Before you went away to school.

MILES: What happened?

The GOVERNESS drops to her knees beside the bed, and reaches out for him.

GOVERNESS: If you *knew* how I want to help you. I'd rather die than hurt a hair of you or do you a wrong. Dear little Miles. I just want you to help me save you!

There's a wild gust of wind. It's as if the rain is inside the room, and the house is shaking. Then several things happen at once. The sound of a sash window crashing and glass smashing. MILES shrieks high and loud – whether of jubilation or terror is unclear. The candle's blown out. Darkness.

(Continued.) The candle's out.

MILES: It was I who blew it, dear.

SCENE THIRTEEN

1840.

The hall.

The following morning.

MRS GROSE: Ah, miss, I've found you. Have you written?

GOVERNESS: Here. *(Holds up sealed, addressed envelope.)*. Have you seen Flora?

MRS GROSE: I thought you carried off both the children after breakfast.

GOVERNESS: I did. But she's slipped away.

MRS GROSE: *(Disparagingly.)* Oh miss…

GOVERNESS: Miles insisted on playing his violin for us, and he somehow contrived to lull me into sleep, and, when I woke, Flora had gone. Perhaps she's with the maids.

MRS GROSE: No, I just passed both the girls on the stairs.

GOVERNESS: Then she's at a distance. She's not given me the slip for any small adventure. She's gone out. To be with *her*!

MRS GROSE: *(Appalled.)* Oh miss…!

GOVERNESS: We must find them. I've a conviction she's returned to the lake. I've always felt she wanted to go back alone. Come.

MRS GROSE: But where's Master Miles?

GOVERNESS: Upstairs still.

MRS GROSE: And you'll leave him unattended?

GOVERNESS: Oh, I strongly suspect he has company enough.

MRS GROSE: You mean –?

GOVERNESS: He's with that devil no doubt, playing to him, enchanting him! But *(About the letter.)* now this is done, I don't mind. *(Laying the sealed letter on the hall table.)* Luke will take it.

MRS GROSE: Wait, miss. You'll go with nothing on?

GOVERNESS: I can't wait to dress. If you must do so, I leave you. *(Exits.)*.

MRS GROSE: *(Looking up.)* Alone with them?

MRS GROSE quickly follows the GOVERNESS off. As soon as they're gone, MILES saunters on, looks about, pockets the letter and exits.

SCENE FOURTEEN

The lake.

Grey, misty and forlorn. The cries of a mournful starling and a lonely raven.

The GOVERNESS and MRS GROSE re-enter.

GOVERNESS: She's taken the boat. She must have used it to go over, and then hidden it.

MRS GROSE: That flat-bottomed boat? The little girl? All alone?

GOVERNESS: She's not alone, and at such times she's not a girl: she's an old, old woman. She'll already be over on the far bank.

The GOVERNESS starts to lead off.

MRS GROSE: And we must walk all the way round?

GOVERNESS: Certainly.

MRS GROSE: Laws!

The GOVERNESS leads MRS GROSE off.

Young FLORA enters. She's been collecting ferns and pebbles, and she sits on the ground to arrange her treasure. The governess and MRS GROSE re-enter and, both seeing her at once, exclaim simultaneously:

GOVERNESS/MRS GROSE: There she is!

FLORA smiles. MRS GROSE falls to her knees to embrace the sitting child. Unsmilingly, FLORA looks over MRS GROSE's shoulder at the governess.

FLORA: *(Her gaiety returning.)* Where are your things – your hat and your coat? And where's Miles?

GOVERNESS: I'll tell *you*, if you'll tell *me*...

FLORA: What?

GOVERNESS: Where, my pet, is Miss Jessel?

MRS GROSE stifles a shriek.

Sound and light create the mood for an apparition. This time, however, no ghost appears. The GOVERNESS sees it out-front. She gasps, seizing MRS GROSE's arm and pointing to the spectre.

(Continued.) She's there, she's there!

The GOVERNESS is not frightened but thrilled at having finally got her proof.

(Continued, to MRS GROSE.) You see? I'm neither cruel nor am I mad. I'm justified!

The GOVERNESS half bows to MISS JESSEL in gratitude.

MRS GROSE gazes to where the GOVERNESS pointed, while the GOVERNESS checks FLORA's reaction. But FLORA is dismayed and doesn't even glance towards the ghost. Instead, she stares at the governess – hard and accusing.

GOVERNESS: *(To FLORA.)* She's there, you unhappy little thing – there, there, *there*, and you see her as well as you see me!

FLORA stares at the GOVERNESS with unflinching reprobation.

MRS GROSE: What a dreadful turn, to be sure, miss! Where on earth do you see anything?

The GOVERNESS grasps MRS GROSE, thrusting her forwards and presenting her to the ghost, pointing all the while.

GOVERNESS: You don't see her exactly as *we* see? You don't now? She's as big as a blazing fire! Only look, dearest woman, *look*!

MRS GROSE looks harder, sees nothing and groans out of pity for the GOVERNESS, and from relief that there is, in fact, no ghost there. In response to which, the GOVERNESS, though she still sees the ghost, feels her situation begin to crumble, gazing hopelessly and desperately at her two companions.

MRS GROSE: *(To FLORA, embracing her protectively.)* She isn't there, little lady, and nobody's there – and you never see nothing, my sweet. How can poor Miss Jessel…when poor Miss Jessel's dead and buried? *We* know, don't we, love? It's all a mistake and a worry and a joke – and we'll go home as fast as we can.

United, FLORA (implacably hard.) and MRS GROSE (horrified.) stand opposed to the governess. It's as though FLORA is both girl and woman when she speaks.

FLORA: I don't know what you mean. I see nobody. I see nothing. I never have. I think you're cruel. I don't like you!

She clings to MRS GROSE.

(Continued.) Take me away, take me away – oh, take me away from *her*!

GOVERNESS: From *me*?

FLORA: From you – from you!

GOVERNESS: I see it! That infernal spirit has instructed you how to outface me. Then I've lost you forever. My God, I'm alone, completely alone. *(To MRS GROSE.)* Go, go!

MRS GROSE obeys. Without interruption, FLORA ages fully, taking us to 1870.

SCENE FIFTEEN

FLORA: What fabrication! What fantasy!

MRS GROSE exits swiftly.

GOVERNESS: What a clever little trick to have cloaked yourself in cheap outrage. You managed to fool Mrs Grose, but not for a minute did you fool me. Now, oh now, Flora, now's the time. Confess it to me now so we may at least live with it and learn what it meant.

FLORA: What it meant? I know precisely what it meant. There was no woman by the lake, anymore than there was a tormented soul in the schoolroom. It was you, all you.

The GOVERNESS's nervous tics have returned.

(Continued.) You, alone in an empty room, shouting at yourself, 'You terrible, miserable woman'!

GOVERNESS: You don't know what I saw. How could you possibly know?

FLORA: I know what *I* saw. Nothing. And I know what I see standing in front of me now. That same 'terrible miserable woman'.

GOVERNESS: What impudence is this?

FLORA: A sad spinster emerged from the shell of a desperate virgin –

GOVERNESS: Don't be revolting!

FLORA: Delirious from lack of sleep, terrified of everything, unable even to dream of such a man for fear of the difference between your station and his – your mind fed by fiction and fantasies – your fevered brain full of Amelias and Clarissas fuelled the images of those who *had* dared to be different, who had dared to love.

Fractured music quietly under, building.

GOVERNESS: How dare you pretend to know me? To talk to me like that? To claim to know who I loved?

FLORA: *You* conjured up the ghosts of Peter Quint and Miss Jessel.

GOVERNESS: *(Grasping FLORA.)* I loved you, Flora. You and Miles. You alone filled my heart.

FLORA: Let me go.

GOVERNESS: No one's ever replaced you in my affections. How could I love when I'd already given my heart to the two of you? I'm not sad or alone. I love! As I've loved since I first saw you. You. You were the ones I risked everything for. You were the ones I willingly, devotedly, offered up my life to save.

FLORA breaks free, pushing the GOVERNESS backwards towards the rocking chair. It starts to rock slowly. The GOVERNESS is drawn to it.

FLORA: We didn't need saving. Can't you see? Don't you understand? There was no danger to us. No danger until *you* arrived.

FLORA turns to go, as we return to 1840, lights changing.

GOVERNESS: Flora, don't leave me here...!

FLORA exits.

The GOVERNESS sits in the rocking chair, cries, rocking, alone.

Act Four

The next day.

The GOVERNESS rocks herself in her chair. She's glassy eyed with a new steely determination. MRS GROSE approaches.

MRS GROSE: I'm afraid, miss, the little lady's hardly slept a wink all night and woke up horribly feverish.

The GOVERNESS is on her feet with renewed vigour.

GOVERNESS: She persists in denying she saw anything yesterday, or that she's ever seen anything?

MRS GROSE: Ah, miss, it isn't a matter which I can push her on. Yet it isn't either as if I much needed to. It's made her, every inch of her, quite…old.

GOVERNESS: Oh, I see her perfectly. She resents, like some high little personage, this slur against her honesty. She's 'respectable', the chit! She'll never speak to me again.

MRS GROSE: Indeed, miss. She asks me every three minutes if I think you're coming in. She's a bundle of nerves, and won't take her eye off the door for fear of you.

FLORA enters to another part of the stage and sits motionless, traumatised.

GOVERNESS: Has she said a single other word about Miss Jessel?

MRS GROSE: Not one. And of course you know, miss, I took it from her, by the lake, that, just then at least, there *was* nobody.

GOVERNESS: And, naturally, you take it from her still.

MRS GROSE: I don't contradict her. What else can I do?

GOVERNESS: Nothing. She's the canniest little person to deal with. Their two friends have made them cleverer even than nature did. Flora has her grievance now, and she'll work it to the end.

MRS GROSE: But to *what* end, miss?

GOVERNESS: She wants to get rid of me.

MRS GROSE: Never again so much as *look* at you!

GOVERNESS: And you've come to speed me on my way. Well, I've a better idea. It's *you* who must go. And take Flora with you.

MRS GROSE: Where in the world –?

GOVERNESS: To their uncle.

MRS GROSE: Only to tell on you?

GOVERNESS: To leave me with my remedy.

MRS GROSE: What's that?

GOVERNESS: Miles. His loyalty. But there's one vital thing: the children mustn't see each other for as much as an instant before her departure.

MRS GROSE glances away. On another part of the stage, MILES enters

(Continued.) Do you mean… They've already met?

MRS GROSE: I'm not such a fool as that, miss. Though she's alone at present, she's locked in safe. And yet…

GOVERNESS: Yet what?

67

MRS GROSE: Is anywhere safe from the little gentleman?

GOVERNESS: Not in the least.

MILES holds out his hand to FLORA. She takes it. They exit together.

(Continued.) I see a chance. I'm resolute and steeled for it. But I need a day or two with him alone, so get off with his sister as soon as possible.

MRS GROSE: You're right. I'll go this morning. It's the place itself – the little lady must leave it. And I can't stay now, miss, not since…

GOVERNESS: You mean, since yesterday, you've seen…?

MRS GROSE: I've heard.

GOVERNESS: Heard?

MRS GROSE: From that little girl – horrors. On my honour, miss, she says things…

GOVERNESS: Oh, thank God.

MRS GROSE: Thank God?

GOVERNESS: It's more proof on my side.

MRS GROSE: It certainly is.

GOVERNESS: She's so horrible?

MRS GROSE: Really shocking.

GOVERNESS: And about me?

MRS GROSE: Since you must have it, yes. It's beyond everything. I can't think where she can have picked up the shocking language.

GOVERNESS: *(Laughs.)* I can.

MRS GROSE: Well, perhaps I ought to, since I've heard some of it before. I'll get her far away from here, and from *them*.

GOVERNESS: She may be different then. She may be free. *(Seizing MRS GROSE with joy.)* Then, in spite of yesterday, you believe –

MRS GROSE: In such doings? I believe.

The GOVERNESS embraces MRS GROSE.

GOVERNESS: There's one thing to remember. My letter will have reached town before you.

MRS GROSE: No it won't. It wasn't where you'd left it when I came back with Miss Flora, but Luke declared he'd neither noticed nor touched it. *(Suddenly.)* You see?

GOVERNESS: Yes. Miles took it.

MRS GROSE: What he must have done at school! Steal letters!

GOVERNESS: *(Ushering MRS GROSE out.)* You go. I'll get it out of him. We'll talk and he'll confess. If he does, he's saved. And if he's saved, then I am.

SCENE TWO.

The drawing room.

MILES: Is Flora really very awfully ill?

GOVERNESS: *(Grander than before.)* Bly has ceased to agree with her.

MILES: Did it disagree with her so terribly suddenly?

GOVERNESS: One had seen it coming. I trust the journey will dissipate the influence and carry it off. And London will set her up again.

MILES: *(Noticing the governess' changed tone.)* Ah, I see, I see.

Like FLORA, MILES has also aged, and now the child is, in some sense, a man.

(Continued.) She's already gone?

GOVERNESS: Indeed. The coach left a few hours ago, while you were out walking.

MILES: Well… So, we're alone.

GOVERNESS: Yes. *(Whimsically.)* Like a young couple on their wedding journey, abandoned together for the first time and suddenly shy. *(Picking up her embroidery.)* But we're not absolutely alone, are we?

MILES: No, we have the others.

GOVERNESS: Indeed, we have the others.

MILES is thinking of the servants, but the GOVERNESS is thinking of the ghosts.

MILES: Yet even though we have them, they don't much count, do they?

GOVERNESS: It depends on what you call much.

MILES: Yes, everything depends.

The GOVERNESS takes her work to the sofa.

Light and sound hint at the materialisation of a ghost in the room – QUINT. As before, there's no physical representation of him. Through the scene, QUINT comes and goes and, each time, the GOVERNESS is alarmed by it and relieved when it departs, convinced she's made it disappear herself.

MILES doesn't notice. He only feels awkward about the conversation – trapped.

MILES: *(With spirit.)* Well, I'm glad Bly agrees with *me.*

GOVERNESS: You've certainly seen a good deal of it today.

MILES: I didn't feel obliged to turn up to the schoolroom. Was I wrong?

GOVERNESS: Of course not. I hope you've been enjoying yourself.

MILES: Yes, I've been ever so far – all round about – miles and miles away. I've never been so free.

GOVERNESS: Do you like it?

MILES: Do *you?*

The ghost retreats.

(Continued.) I hope you don't mind particularly being alone with me.

GOVERNESS: Mind? Though I've renounced all claim to your company – I've nothing left to teach you – I still greatly enjoy it. What else should I stay on for?

MILES: You stay on just for *that?*

GOVERNESS: And from the tremendous interest I take in you – till something more worth-your-while can be organised. That needn't surprise you. *(Her voice shaking with emotion.)* Don't you remember how I told you, the night of the storm, that there was nothing in the world I wouldn't do for you?

MILES: Yes. *(Laughing.)* Only that, I think, was to get me to do something for *you.*

GOVERNESS: It was, partly. But you didn't do it.

MILES: You wanted me to tell you something.

GOVERNESS: That's it. Straight out. *(Appearing to concentrate on her work.)* What you have on your mind, you know.

MILES: So *that's* what you've stayed over for.

GOVERNESS: I may as well make a clean breast of it. It was precisely for that.

MILES: Do you mean now? Here?

GOVERNESS: There couldn't be a better place or time.

MILES, anxious, looks round.

(Continued.) You want so greatly to go out again?

MILES: *(Smiling.)* Awfully. I'll tell you everything – I mean anything you like. You'll stay with me, and we shall both be all right, and I'll tell you – I will. But not now.

GOVERNESS: Why not now?

MILES: *(Lying.)* I have to see Luke.

GOVERNESS: *(Aware he's lying.)* Well, go to Luke, then, and I'll wait. Only, in return, before you leave, satisfy one very much smaller request.

MILES: *Very* much smaller –?

GOVERNESS: *(As off-hand as she can manage.)* Tell me if you took, you know, my letter from the hall table.

Once more, sound and light indicate QUINT's presence. It's more obtrusive than before. The GOVERNESS grabs MILES to protect him. She draws him close, instinctively keeping his back to where she sees QUINT.

MILES: *(Misinterpreting her physicality.)* Very well, I'll tell you, I'll tell you! Yes – I took it.

She embraces MILES, holding him to her breast, shielding him from the sight of QUINT whose progress she follows. Held tightly, MILES struggles for breath.

GOVERNESS: What did you take it for?

MILES: To see what you said about me.

GOVERNESS: You opened the letter?

MILES: I opened it.

Holding him away from her, she inspects his face. He's sweating, terrified – of her, not the ghost. She thinks his expression is a sign that he is aware of QUINT.

QUINT withdraws. Sound and light restore to normal.

GOVERNESS: And you found nothing!

MILES: *(Shaking his head.)* Nothing.

GOVERNESS: *(Shouting joyfully.)* Nothing, nothing!

MILES: Nothing, nothing.

She kisses his forehead.

GOVERNESS: Is that what you did at school?

MILES: *(Dizzy.)* At school?

GOVERNESS: Did you take letters? Other things?

MILES: *(Affronted.)* Did I *steal*?

GOVERNESS: Was it for that you mightn't go back?

MILES: Oh, did you know I mightn't go back?

GOVERNESS: I know everything. So, did you…?

MILES: No, I didn't steal.

GOVERNESS: *(Shaking MILES in frustration.)* Then what did you do?

MILES: I…said things.

GOVERNESS: Only that?

MILES: They thought it was enough.

GOVERNESS: To turn you out?

MILES: Well, I suppose I oughtn't.

GOVERNESS: But to whom did you say these things?

MILES: I don't know.

GOVERNESS: Was it to everyone?

MILES: No, it was only to – I don't remember their names.

GOVERNESS: Were they so many?

MILES: Only a few. Those I liked.

The GOVERNESS lets go of MILES and he retreats from her.

GOVERNESS: And did they repeat what you said?

MILES: *(Moving further away, still breathless, feeling cornered.)* Oh, yes, they must have repeated it. To those *they* liked.

GOVERNESS: And it came round to the masters?

MILES: Yes. But I didn't know they'd tell.

GOVERNESS: They didn't – they've never told.

MILES: Then I suppose it was too bad.

GOVERNESS: Too bad?

MILES: What I said. Too bad for the school to write home in a letter.

GOVERNESS: What *were* these things?

Again, sound (more discordant and unsettling) and light (more strange and threatening) indicate the return of QUINT, and, again, the governess protectively grabs hold of MILES. The effect builds to the scene's end.

(To QUINT.) No more, no more, no more!

MILES: Is she here?!

GOVERNESS: She?!

MILES: Miss Jessel!

GOVERNESS: You talked to Flora?! No, it's not her. But it's straight before us. It's *there* – the coward horror!

MILES: It's he?

GOVERNESS: Who do you mean by 'he'?

MILES: Peter Quint – you devil! *(He's straining to see, but she continues to hold him tight.)* Where?!

GOVERNESS: What does he matter now, my own? What will he ever matter? I have you, and he has lost you forever! There, there!

MILES, desperate to identify the ghost, sees nothing. He kicks and bites, trying anything to wriggle loose from her. His teeth get a purchase on the inside of her left wrist. She screams in pain but holds him tighter. He cries out and finally gets loose, but she (her passion providing extra power and agility) immediately recaptures him, clutching him still tighter, eyes fixed on QUINT, unaware she's suffocating the boy.

(Continued.) No more! No more! No more, no more, no more...

MILES is struggling for survival. Sound reaches a horrifying climax while lights focus down on MILES and the GOVERNESS, burning intensely bright. After a time, his limbs drop lifelessly as he dies in her arms. Sound and light are restored to normal, indicating that QUINT has gone.

The GOVERNESS turns to MILES, releasing him slowly, but she can't understand what she sees.

SCENE THREE

1870

The GOVERNESS continues to hold the dead boy in her arms.

GOVERNESS: He jerked straight round. He stared, he glared at Quint, and he saw –

FLORA: Nothing. The stupid shrubs and dull things of November through the window.

GOVERNESS: He uttered a cry. It sounded like a creature hurled over an abyss. And I grasped him to me, as if I was catching him as he fell. I caught him, yes. And I held him with such a passion. But at the end of a minute I began to feel what it truly was that I held. We were alone with the quiet day, and his little heart, dispossessed, had stopped.

FLORA: Was he really ever possessed?

GOVERNESS: Dispossessed of life, I mean.

FLORA: Or, rather, just a boy, and guiltless.

GOVERNESS: No, for if *he* were guiltless…

She draws breath sharply as a new realisation dawn.

(Continued.) Then… I…

She begins to understand that she has murdered MILES. She looks up at FLORA with growing horror, while FLORA's face starts to reflect a grim satisfaction. FLORA has finally discovered what happened to MILES, and, in doing so, achieved her revenge, because, from now on, the GOVERNESS will be forced to bear the guilt.

Lights slowly fade out.

THE END

Tim Luscombe's first play was *EuroVision*, produced by Sir Andrew Lloyd Webber at the Vaudeville Theatre in 1994 starring Anita Dobson and James Dreyfus. More recently, he's written for the National Theatre Studio (*The Schuman Plan*), the Royal Court (*The One You Love*), the Orange Tree (*Hungry Ghosts*) and the Hampstead Theatre. *Pig* was produced at the Buddies in Bad Times in Toronto in 2013, *A Map of the Region* was shortlisted for Manchester Royal Exchange's Bruntwood Prize in 2011, and his adaptation of Henry James's *The Turn of the Screw* toured the UK in 2018. All four of Tim's Jane Austen adaptations (*Northanger Abbey, Persuasion, Mansfield Park* and *Emma*) have met with success. *Emma* premiered in the summer of 2017 and went on to tour the UK. *Persuasion* was produced at the Salisbury Playhouse in 2011, *Mansfield Park* was toured by The Production Exchange from the Theatre Royal Bury St Edmunds in 2012 and 2013, and *Northanger Abbey* has been seen in many venues up and down England over the past ten years. It was revived in Chicago in 2013 and enjoyed another successful British tour in 2017. *Persuasion* and *Mansfield Park* are published by Oberon. As a director, Tim's productions have been seen in the West End of London and in New York – on Broadway *(Artist Descending a Staircase* at the Helen Hayes*)* and Off Broadway *(When she Danced* at the Playwright's Horizons*)*. London directorial credits include *Easy Virtue* (Garrick.), *Private Lives* (starring Joan Collins at the Aldwych.), *Artist Descending a Staircase* (Duke of York's), *EuroVision* (Vaudeville*)*, *The One You Love* (Ambassadors), *Relative Values* (Savoy), *Snow Orchid* (starring Jude Law and Paola Dionisotti at the Gate Theatre), *When She Danced* at the King's Head and *The Green Bay Tree* at the Jermyn Street Theatre. *The Green Bay* Tree, edited by Tim, is also published by Oberon. Tim was nominated for a Lawrence Olivier Award for his work as a director on productions of *Easy Virtue* and *The Browning Version & Harlequinade.*

For more information please see www.timluscombe.com